Hell's Marshal

Book One in the Hell's Butcher Series

Chris Barili

Hell's Marshal

Formatting by Rik - Wild Seas Formatting
(http://www.WildSeasFormatting.com)
Cover art by Michelle Johnson of Blue Sky Design
Edited by Jennifer Severino

Printed in the United States of America

ACKNOWLEDGMENTS

They say it takes a village to raise a child, and they also say that a book is like an author's offspring. So it stands to reason that it takes a village — or more precisely a kind of extended family — to write a book. I'd like to thank the members of that extended family, without whom Frank Butcher and his posse would never have hit the page.

First of all to my wife, Jennifer, and my kids, who had to put up with my endless hours researching, brainstorming, plotting, writing, revising, griping, complaining, and drinking: I love you all. I do this because you all inspire me.

To Russell Davis, who taught me to write outside my box and Michaela Roessner, who made me write inside some very tight ones. And to my cohorts from Western — you guys keep me going when I'm ready to give up, and you keep writer's solitude from becoming isolation.

Finally, since I wasn't around in 1892, I turned to the following expert historians to make sure the basic facts about my settings were straight. They're all volunteers, by the way, doing the yeoman's work of keeping our past alive that we might learn and thus not repeat its mistakes:

Bob Seago and Johanna Gray, Creede Historical Society, Creede, CO

Hayes Scriven, Executive Director, Northfield Historical Society, Northfield, MN

James Thorn, Clay County Museum, Clay County, MO

Christopher Harris, Resident Historian, Clay County Archives, Clay County, MO

CHAPTER ONE

Turned out Hell looked a lot like a jail cell, only with bars of fire and a mattress stuffed with shards of glass. Frank Butcher hated the time he spent in his cell, even though the only alternative was the pit of fire they threw him in for punishment on a regular basis. At least he felt like he deserved those periods of horrific and agonizing pain, like they were just punishment for the things he'd done. For the people he'd killed.

One in particular. For Ron.

In the fires, only sheer agony and terror filled his mind, eclipsing all else and making it impossible to even think. Here, in the broiling cell, his mind had space to wander, to make trips back to the things he'd done that put him here. That was the Devil's way of torturing him, by dragging him back to the past and making him relive the most horrible of his deeds. A constant reminder he'd hurt people, robbed innocents of their lives, and killed the one person he, as a father, should never have harmed.

The fires cleansed him of those memories, wiped him clean for however long they lasted—Hell stole his sense of time—but returning to his cell always re-caked his soul with the filth of murder.

No, Frank would take the searing, purging agony of the fire pit over this any day.

He paced the confines of his six-by-ten rectangular prison, his boot heels clacking on the hard floor. After taking off his leather gloves, he ran his fingers through the burning bars just to remind himself that pain still existed. Pain worked differently here—his body had died, so pain should have too—but he didn't care. As long as he could suffer.

Frank trudged to his bed and flopped onto the mattress. Pain erupted in his back as sharp glass edges and points shredded his skin, ensuring every inch of his back was cut. The sticky warmth of his own blood oozed into the material, causing it to cling to him when he shifted. The discomfort filled a hole in his heart.

He stared at his forearm, at the fleshy latticework of scars there, a net of painful reminders. Frank discovered the act of slicing himself by accident. While stalking his cell, tortured by his memories and guilt, he'd brushed his arm against a nail in his bed frame, and for that frozen instant, his pain had been all physical, his mind momentarily free of its torture and suffering while it focused on the physical pain.

He'd started using the nail, intentionally rubbing his arm on it to draw blood and cause pain. Only surface wounds, but at first, they were enough. Soon, though, his internal anguish overpowered the minor pain, and Frank needed more, something deeper. So he'd taken a shard of glass from the mattress and sliced the back of his arm, pressing deep and wincing, almost crying out, while the sharp edge bit through skin and flesh.

Now he had scars everywhere, not just his arms. His chest, his thighs, his calves, hands, and feet. A mesh of thin scars—the wounds healed overnight here—connected pain from one part of his body to another, uniting him in a network of suffering, a web of sorrow.

Frank's mind wandered for a moment, allowing the image of a boy to fill his vision, a boy with dark skin and a hook nose, but eyes that could only be Frank's. The boy—just short of a man, really—gazed up at Frank while a puddle of blood grew under his head, soaking into the dirt. Frank's heart broke all over again as he watched his son die.

Something skittered in the pitch black outside his cell, an insect sound, saving him from the pit of despair he'd fallen into.

They were coming for him. Finally.

The sound neared his cell, a clacking of chitin on granite—or whatever the floors of Hell were made of. A moment later, a pair of black antennae poked in through the flaming bars.

Part cockroach and part human, Damon's hard outer shell ticked on the floor as he rose up on the rear of his six legs. He wiggled his antennae, searching for Frank. His human face was puffy and swollen, and he never opened his eyes anymore, preferring the senses of the bug with which Hell had fused him.

"Frank Butcher?" he asked, his feelers waving in Frank's face.

"You know it's me, Damon. You know everyone here.

Let's go. I need the pain."

Damon flinched back from the bars as if their flames had somehow hurt him.

"No fffire pit for you," he hissed.

Frank stepped back from the bars, apprehensive. This was supposed to be his fate for all eternity. There'd never been a deviation before. Why now?

"What are you talking about? Is this some kind of trick?"

He'd never known the bug-man to make a joke.

Damon rubbed his front legs together as his middle ones unlocked Frank's cell. "They want to sssee you."

Frank retreated to the predictable pain of his cot, resisting the urge to curl into a ball on the glass-filled mat.

"Who?" In his heart, he already knew and was hoping Damon would prove him wrong.

"The judgesss."

"What the Hell do they want?"

Damon shrugged with his two pairs of free legs.

Frank turned his back on the jailer. "Then tell them they already judged me. They don't get to do it twice."

"It's not your choiccce. Disssobey them at your own risssk."

Frank shot him a glare over his shoulder. "What more could they possibly do to me? Tell the judges I said to piss off."

Damon made a tsking sound, and Frank heard him open the door.

"Very well," said the jailer. "Hul will make you."

Frank whirled, but an instant too late, as iridescent tendrils whipped around his arms and legs, shooting bullets of fire through his extremities and into his chest. Before him stood Hul, a featureless creature, roughly the shape of a man, but with dozens of finger-like, glowing tentacles sprouting from each shoulder. As they attached themselves to Frank's body, each one sent a jolt of agony through his spine.

An instant later, Frank lost control of himself, his arms thrashing and jerking, his legs dancing an obscene jig. He fought for command over his body, but every time he did, tiny shocks pulsed into him.

"Ssstop resisssting," Damon ordered. "Hul will make it worse if you fight him."

Frank fought a moment longer, but fatigue rushed over him and he gave in. To his surprise, he didn't fall. Instead, he walked, in spasmodic jerks and movements. Frightened, he struggled again, only to be rewarded with a series of shocks that left his limbs feeling like jelly and his mind scattered.

He surrendered again, and stepped through the open door. Damon started off down the pitch black corridor, his feet clicking on the floor. Hul moved behind Frank, and compelled him to follow. Frank didn't resist, couldn't any longer. His will belonged to the being behind him, the combination of man and Man O' War who served as Hell's torturer. As if they needed one.

"Looks like I'll go see the judges," he muttered. "Tell them to piss off myself."

Somewhere ahead of him, Damon's chuckle hissed through the darkness.

CHAPTER TWO

Frank felt like a marionette as he moved herky-jerky down the corridor. The only light came from the glowing Hul, and even that seemed to soak into the walls and floor, making Frank rely on his puppet-master for direction. Twice, he tripped on unseen obstacles, once whacking his shin so hard he cried out.

Hul stopped him and Frank found himself facing a dark, steel-bound double door with no visible knobs or latches.

"This isn't the courtroom," he muttered. The last time he'd seen the three judges had been at his own hearing, when he'd been absolved of his crimes but opted for eternity in Hell anyway, his guilt too deep and ingrained for him to ever forgive himself.

"The courtroom wasss in the underworld, Frank

Butcher. Thisss is Hell—The Bossss makes the rulesss down here."

Frank shrugged. "I don't suppose I'm meeting the head honcho, am I?"

"Just the judgesss. Big Bossss doesn't know about thisss, and you'd bessst keep it that way."

Damon opened the left hand door, its hinges creaking up and down the corridor. Cold air whooshed from the room as if it was a sealed crypt, and the stink of death assailed Frank's senses.

The tentacles released their grip and all Frank's strength fled him. He fell to his knees as a hundred sparks of lightning flashed across his skin. Gasping for air, as if his entire body had depended on Hul's power to live, he fought the urge to retch.

Control returned to him bit-by-bit, and he rose to his feet. He thought about running, but one look at Hul's iridescent body told him he would shock Frank into submission at the first sign of flight. So Frank faced the door and took a deep breath before entering the chamber.

The judges sat at a long, wooden table, shrouded in darkness except for the flickering orange light of a fire behind them. They looked as frightening as they had the last time he'd seen them. Even seated, they were taller than Frank, looming shadows whose presence made the dark, cavernous room feel like there was no space for anyone or anything else. On the left sat Bill Hickok, his hat tilted to the left over the tangled brown ropes of his hair, his long moustache moving of its own accord, a living thing stuck under his hawkish nose. His eyes stared a cold blue. On the right, Morgan Earp's moustache looked fairly normal, except for the fact that it ended in flames that flickered and jumped. A six shooter gleamed black on the table before him, and his glowing green eyes locked on Frank.

And in the middle, red eyes burning into Frank's, sat Marshal John Webber, who Frank had shot and left for the wolves outside Fort Dodge. One of four unjust kills in Frank's long career of killing. Webber hummed with rage, his oily goatee turned down around his perpetual snarl of a mouth. His hate for Frank oozed from every pore.

"Let it go," Frank muttered, wishing he had his six-shooter on his hip. "If you'd been a better marshal, you'd have gone up instead of down."

Pain erupted in Frank's temples, driving him to his knees again. Even though his head felt like it might burst, he refused to let them hear him scream.

"Frank Butcher." Their voices came as one, each layered atop the other, like some ghastly chorus of death. "You must learn respect. Now, rise."

The pain winked out, leaving Frank to wobble to his feet.

"We require something of you, Frank Butcher." Earp spoke alone this time, something Frank had never heard before. "We need someone with your skills. There's been an escape."

Frank paused. "An escape from where?"

The three conferred, a chorus of faint hisses, making Frank's stomach do a flip. When they finished, Hickok spoke alone.

"An escape from Hell." He brushed back a grungy lock of hair as if it were elegant, and fidgeted with his suit coat. "A soul has broken free and now roams the mortal world."

"How's that possible?"

More hissing, then Webber's crimson glare turned Frank's knees weak, his gut twisting at the sound of the marshal's pinched voice.

"We sent this soul to do our bidding in the underworld. Instead, he took possession of a mortal body and now he wreaks havoc in the living realm."

Frank scratched the stubble on his chin. "I thought Hell's Boss-man enjoyed havoc."

"He doesn't know about this," Hickok whispered. Frank wasn't sure whispering hid anything from the guy who ran Hell. "We sent this soul abroad on our own. We must keep his escape a secret from The Prince."

Frank detected the slightest tremble in Hickok's voice and tucked it in the saddlebags of his mind for later use. While the judges ruled the underworld, they answered to higher powers.

"So, how does this involve me?"

"You will bring him back to Hell," Earp said, like Frank didn't have a choice. "Quietly."

Frank crossed his arms over his chest. "And why would I do that?"

"Do not try our patience," Webber said, his eyes flaring. He grinned, showing fangs where they hadn't been before. "We can double or triple your suffering."

Frank laughed in their faces. "You think increasing my punishment will make me do what you want? Gimme your worst, then, boys. Make me suffer like no one's ever suffered before."

This time, the judges' hissing conversation carried a hesitant note of uncertainty. Doubt.

"Perhaps we misjudged you," said Hickok, his voice more eloquent than the other two. "If you do this for us, we will grant you absolution. We will cleanse your soul of all its sin and send you somewhere you can forget the past. Your agony will end."

"You don't learn real fast, do you?" Frank snapped. "I want to suffer, I need to. I killed my father, and my own son! I deserve—"

"Silence!" the judges bellowed as one. "It is not your place to decide what you deserve. We passed judgment on you and found you forgiven, but you rejected our authority. You should not be here, Frank Butcher!"

Webber leaned forward, his red eyes burning. "Now, you're going to do what we command you or we'll reduce the time you spend in The Pit. We'll be sure you sit in your cell for the rest of time."

Frank started to object, but Webber raised a finger in front of his face. "And I will take away every sharp object you can use to hurt yourself, so all you can do is sit there and remember the people you killed. Especially your boy."

He had Frank cornered like a wild colt in a stall, and Frank knew it.

"Who am I looking for, then?"

Webber leaned back and studied Frank from under the brim of his hat. His eyes lost some of their heat.

"We need you to bring back this particular soul," he explained.

An image of a man's face materialized in the air in front of Frank, making him jump back a step. He ignored the hissed snicker from Webber and studied the ethereal face before him. A square jaw tapered to a pointed chin, with thin lips that sneered with the arrogance of self-righteousness. Cruel, blue eyes stared out cold under slicked-back hair the color of sand. Frank recognized the killer in an instant.

"You let Jesse James escape from Hell? No wonder you don't want The Boss-man to know. James was a cold-blooded killer."

All three fixed him with withering glares.

"We know his sins." Hickok said. "We condemned

him to Hell for them. Can you bring him back?"

"That depends on what bringing a soul back to Hell entails, I reckon."

The face of Jesse James faded from sight.

"First, you will need to find him," Earp said. "We think he's set on causing trouble in Clay County, Missouri, but we last detected him in Colorado."

"Don't recall him doing any heists in the Colorado territory," Frank said. "You sure he's there?"

"Positive." Earp's long moustache twitched, imp-like flames dancing as he spoke. "Near a place called Creede."

"How do I find him?"

"He won't look like himself," Webber said. "He has taken possession of a body in the living world. Look for someone acting oddly. Speaking in tongues, hurting people. He could be anyone."

"Sounds like a demon," Frank said.

"He's not a demon," Hickok said, "but the signs are similar."

"I see. So, what next?"

"The soul cannot pass from the living world straight to Hell," Earp said. "It must pass through the underworld. His underworld, created from his nightmares. We'll take it from there."

Frank remembered his own underworld, where he had to face his own sins again, do battle with his own inner demons. It was that way for all who passed through — everyone faced a nightmare world built from the dark shadows of their hearts and minds, and if they managed to correct their errors, they were forgiven.

No one but Frank had ever chosen eternal damnation over absolution.

"And how do I send him there?"

"You must drive the spirit from its living host," all

three said at once. "You can do this through use of certain religious practices, but it is not easy and requires a holy man. Since you're a denizen of Hell, no priest will help you."

"All right, so exorcism is out. How else?"

"You must kill the body, then use talismans we give you to send the spirit to the underworld. If you fail to send it across, it will simply possess another body."

Bill Hickok spoke alone. "He may use people from the world of the living to do his dirty work. They'll be his puppets as long as he needs them. Harm as few as possible to keep things quiet."

Frank stood, fists at his sides, taking slow, deep breaths. He hated being backed into a corner, but they'd done it nonetheless. He locked eyes with Webber.

"Why me? Out of all the souls you got down here, why pick me?"

Webber never looked away, the corners of his mouth turning up and his eyes smoldering.

"We have a history, you and me."

So, it was personal. Frank could understand that, at least.

"One condition. If I do this, you increase my time in the pit so it's what I deserve."

The judges conferred, hissing.

"Agreed," they said as one.

Frank nodded. "If I'm gonna be Hell's Marshal, shouldn't I get a badge?"

Webber grinned and a bolt of lightning shot down from the ceiling, crashing into Frank's chest. His body went rigid, and a searing agony blazed on his chest. Fire arced through his body, making his muscles contract until he felt his bones straining not to snap. He tried to scream, but couldn't open his mouth even an inch.

The acrid stink of burning flesh filled his nostrils as the skin on his chest sizzled and cooked like bacon over a fire.

An instant later, the lightning disappeared and Frank collapsed to the floor. When he finally mustered the strength to lift his head, a marshal's badge had been burned in swollen, pink flesh where the lightning had touched him. In the center of the six-pointed star, a skull stared out, flames dancing in the hollows of its eyes. The words "Hell's Marshal" circled it all. The judges faded from sight, snickering as they disappeared.

"Send Jesse James back to us, Marshal Butcher," echoed their voices. "Dead or dead."

CHAPTER THREE

Frank looked around the tiny chamber where Damon and Hul had left him. Nothing. Just four gray walls, a gray floor, and the swirling pinks, purples, and grays of the underworld sky, starless and bleak. He stretched out his arms and touched his fingertips to the walls on either side of him, both too tall and smooth to climb out. Not that he wanted to run around the desert of his personal underworld. He'd seen it once and didn't want to ever again.

No, he'd be better off in the tiny room until someone came along.

As if reading his thoughts, the wall in front of him dissolved from sight and Frank stood in a long, narrow chamber with closed cabinets lining either wall. At the far end, a man in a white coat leaned over a tall table, his back to Frank and his head bowed so Frank could only see the halo of white hair around a shiny bald spot the size of an apple. The man waved Frank forward with an age-spotted hand, not even looking up from his work.

"Come here, Mr. Butcher." His voice buzzed like lightning trapped in a bottle. "I need to issue your gear to you before you head on out. And give you your team, too."

Frank walked forward, placing himself just off center from the old man, hoping to get a look at his face. But all he saw was a scruffy black stubble on his jawline.

"I work alone," he told the man.

The old man chuckled but didn't look up from his work.

Frank took one step closer and stood looking down at his own body, spread out in death's repose. His eyes stared at the sky, cold and blue like ice, and the thin, pink line of a scar ran down his cheek. A forest of stubble stood on the harsh angle of his jaw, while blood and grime caked his straw-colored hair.

A circle of blood stained the white cotton shirt in which they'd buried him.

"What are you doing to my body?" Frank asked.

"This isn't your body," the old man said. "Your real body's been rotting in the ground in Tombstone for two years now. Extensive damage. This is an underworld representation of how it used to look."

"For what?" Frank narrowed his eyes at the old man's hunched back.

"I'm making a pattern, so it'll know how to rebuild itself when you possess it again."

As he turned around, Frank reached for the six-gun he didn't have.

The old man had the face of a fly, with giant,

shimmering eyes of blue, green, and silver. The stubble on his jawline covered much of his face, consisting of thick, black hairs. And his mouth was made up of long, rigid mandibles, suitable for shoveling slop or rotten things inside.

He offered a hand—a normal, human hand. "Name's Thaddeus Slater. But most folks call me Buzzy."

Frank shook his hand, unable to take his eyes off the hideous face before him.

"It isn't polite to stare," Buzzy said, not turning away.

"Sorry," Frank said. "Just…"

"Yeah, I'm ugly as Hell. Literally."

Uncomfortable, Frank changed the subject. "So, I'm using my old body in the living world?"

Buzzy nodded. "Your…prey used a living body, but you can't do that. Judges' orders. So you'll be placed back in your old, rotting corpse. Your body won't really be alive, at least not as you know the word. We call it 'reanimated' instead. It'll rebuild itself in a few days, faster with rest, but you'll have to keep covered up or out of sight until it does. You think I'm ugly, try looking at someone who's been dead two years."

Frank shrugged. "I ain't goin' there to dance with the ladies."

"You don't want to stand out. People see a corpse walking the streets, word's likely to get around. Giving Mr. James advance notice won't help your odds."

Frank saw his point. "Anything else?"

"Don't eat. Your body will rebuild its exterior to match this pattern, but it won't function right. Eating will hog-tie your insides. It's your soul maintaining the re-animation, not normal body functions, so eating will only make a mess of things. You'll breathe just to maintain appearances, but your heart will never beat again."

"Can't drink?"

"Not even water."

"Damn, I was hoping for a whiskey."

Buzzy darted to a cabinet, Frank following.

"You can't bring back his soul without some help."

He jerked open a door on one of the closer cabinets. Inside sat a box of Colt .45 caliber bullets, a rope, a set of shiny steel wrist irons, and a cheap-looking bottle of whiskey with a hooker on the label. Buzzy picked up the rope, tying it quickly into a lasso.

"All these items are made to help you send Jesse James' soul back to the underworld, where the judges can deal with him." He spun the lasso's loop over his head, bringing it down around Frank's neck. "If you can rope him with this lariat, it'll pull the spirit from the host body, keeping it hostage until you get back here."

"I'm no rancher. I can't use one of those."

Buzzy's hands flew over the rope in blurs.

"You might be more familiar with this knot."

Frank lifted the rope from his shoulders, frowning at the hangman's noose the older man had tied.

"Won't that kill the host?"

"They all kill the host. Only exorcism keeps them alive, though usually not much more than a potted plant."

Frank turned to hide his grimace, but the other man had seen it.

"Oh, did you think you'd be saving the victim? Whoever they are, they're already good as dead, Frank. A shell of who they used to be, nothing more than an empty husk holding his soul. Once you're tainted with that kind of evil, nothing can save you."

He pulled the whiskey bottle out and handed it to Frank.

"If you can get him to drink even a drop of this, it'll

capture his soul in the bottle until you bring him back. That might be tricky, though, since it'll capture you, too, if you drink it. And he'll be suspicious if you won't drink with him."

"What if I pour it on him? Break the bottle on his head or something?"

Buzzy shook his head. "It'll hurt real bad for a minute—the whiskey has Holy Water in it—but then he'll just be mad as a hornet. You gotta get it inside him."

Frank nodded and made a mental note.

Next, Buzzy handed him the gleaming wrist irons. They didn't come with a key.

"Let me guess," he said, "slap these on the host and they drive the spirit out."

Buzzy shook his head. "Opposite. Traps the spirit in the body so it can't leave when you…uh…"

He made a finger gun and pointed it at Frank's head.

"Until I kill the victim. Seems like I'm more of an executioner than a marshal."

Buzzy looked Frank in the eye. "You do have a certain reputation. Your skill set suits this mission perfectly."

"You needed a killer, not a lawman."

"Not me, friend. The judges."

Frank shrugged. "Then a killer is what they'll get."

Finally, Buzzy handed Frank the box of bullets. Frank opened it and found one bullet inside.

"That's a last resort weapon," Buzzy said. "Only use it if you have no other choice."

Frank narrowed his eyes. "Why?"

The old man shifted on his feet. It was a subtle movement, one Frank might have missed had he blinked, but it happened.

"You see, this one bullet won't contain a soul, or incapacitate it. Won't knock it out or return it to the underworld. This bullet will destroy the soul, burn it out of existence and leave a gaping hole in the universe where it used to be. It'll stop James' reign of terror in the living world, but destroying a soul makes a lot of noise down here in the underworld, and in—"

He let the sentence hang there between them.

"And in Hell, too?"

Buzzy nodded.

"So the Boss-man will find out?" Frank pressed.

Another nod.

"So, when *should* I use this magic bullet?"

"Never."

Frank gave him a flat stare.

"Then why the Sam-Hell are you giving it to me?"

Buzzy closed the now-empty cabinet and moved back to the examining table to look at Frank's body there.

"Mr. James may try to bring others across to help him. Use that bullet then and only then."

Frank was about to ask more when a door opened in the otherwise smooth, granite wall and an Indian walked in. He was only half Indian—the top half, to be precise—while the bottom half was that of a coyote, with scruffy brown-and-gray fur and a matted tail. His top half was naked but for beads around his upper arms and war paint on his angular face.

The Indian grinned, a wide, crooked smile that spoke of mischief and deception. He raised one hand in greeting, a gesture Frank did not return.

"Batcho," Frank said, jaw tightening. "What the Hell are you doing here?"

The guide stopped a few feet from Frank, his smile fading from his dark face.

"Batcho is going with you, Frank," said Buzzy. "He's part of your little posse."

"No." Frank turned his back on them. "Not him."

"What did I do?" Batcho asked. "I helped you through the underworld, Frank Butcher. I guided you, offered advice. I—"

Frank wheeled, putting his nose just an inch from the Indian's.

"You lied to me every step of the way!" He jabbed his finger at the Indian's chest as he spoke. "You tried to keep me from passing every test. If I'd listened to you, I'd be-"

"Exactly where you are anyway. In Hell."

Frank tried to think of an argument, but the guide was right. He'd lived up to his reputation as a Coyote, playing tricks, but in the end, changing little.

"You have no choice, anyway," Buzzy said. "Judges' orders."

Frank sighed and spit on the floor. "This time, Indian, no lying. Don't send me on any wild goose chases."

Batcho nodded, his broad grin returning. "I promise, if geese need chasing, I'll do it."

Frank raised an eyebrow at him and Batcho cleared his throat.

"Besides, Frank Butcher, we won't be in the underworld, so I will be...different. It is hard to explain."

Frank shrugged, then thought of something and turned to face the red man again.

"You best not be answering to Judge Webber this time."

Batcho blushed and his tail went between his legs. "This time, I answer to all three judges. They ordered me to guide you well."

Frank studied him a moment longer, saw no hint of deception in his deep, dark eyes, and nodded.

"I suppose we'd better get going, then."

"You will have more help once you reach the world

of the living," said Buzzy, as he led them toward the door. "We sent the other two members of your little posse ahead to do some scouting. They'll meet you there."

Frank's hackles rose. "Who else is involved in this little shindig?"

Buzzy looked away, while Batcho shrugged and shook his head. "They didn't tell me."

Buzzy returned his gaze to Frank, his face apologetic. "You will find out in due time, Mr. Butcher." His eyes glittered in the wavering light from outside the door, and his mandibles clicked in anticipation. "Your stage is waiting. Please, there's little time to waste. James has already started to kill. Before long, The Boss-man will find out."

"Then there'll be Hell to pay," Batcho said. "Literally."

Frank gave him a deadpan look and stepped out the door into the painted dusk of the underworld desert. An all-black stagecoach waited, its long-dead horses kicking and snorting, stirring up clouds of red and purple dust from the road. Their eyes glowed red as embers.

Frank shivered as he saw the driver, a shadowy figure in a long, black duster, a black bandana covering his face. Yellow eyes peered out from under his wide-brimmed hat, locked on Frank and Batcho.

The dead stare took Frank back to his first trip into the underworld, when the same driver had pushed him into the burning Colorado River. It had been just one of many painful, agonizing moments for Frank during his testing. The testing that had wrongly found him absolved of his sins. The testing he'd defied to end up in Hell.

He tipped his hat and even though the driver didn't move, the sound of a whip split the air, telling him it was time to go.

"He going with us?" Frank asked Batcho.

The guide shook his head, black hair flying. "He cannot remain in the living world. He must guide others on their underworld journeys."

Frank glanced at the driver one last time, then mounted the coach.

"We'd best get a move on."

CHAPTER FOUR

The stage stopped so suddenly, it tossed Frank out of his seat and onto his knees. Beside him, Batcho seemed unfazed, simply rolling his chin down a bit, then turning a mischievous smile on Frank. He leaned his head out the window and spoke to the driver in a muffled voice.

When he pulled his head back inside, concern wrinkled the brown expanse of his forehead.

"The driver wanted me to warn you," he said. "This part can be a bit…difficult. We will be traveling from the underworld to the realm of the living. A kind of wall divides the two, and crossing it is not easy, especially going this direction. Coming back, all you have to do is die, but this way, you must live. And living is always harder than dying."

Frank shifted in his seat. "What's it like?"

The Indian shrugged and closed the blinds on both windows. "It's my first time returning to life, too. No matter what you hear, don't look out the window."

Frank groaned, but had time for little more, as the coach pitched ahead, throwing him back into his seat. As they gathered speed, ethereal sounds, like distant singing, reached in, nudging Frank to open the blinds and find their source. Batcho covered his ears as howling arose, chanting in his native tongue, as if his voice could block out the sounds.

The wind whistled by, and voices emerged, carried on it like leaves or dust. They grew into screams, wails of agony and terror so filled with grief, it almost brought him to tears.

Next came words, voices he knew, but could not name, pleading with him to open the window, to peek outside for just an instant. His heart longed to do so, even as the stage continued to accelerate, racing across the desert like a train. All he could think about was opening the shade and looking outside. He knew these voices, after all. Trusted them more than the dark and foreboding stage driver.

Finally, it just became too much. Frank's willpower caved and he threw open the shade. Purple light splashed into the coach, mingled with red, yellow, and orange, casting strange, oblong shadows on Batcho's face.

Frank marveled at the sights outside, at the shifting colors of the sky, the jagged mountains to their right, rising like dragons in the distance. Faces appeared in thin air, people whose names he'd forgotten, their mouths all open in horrified screams as they rushed along beside the coach.

One — a blond woman with red-painted lips and bug-like lashes — opened her eyes wide and pointed ahead of the coach. Frank followed her direction and regretted it.

The stage rushed across the desert, streaking over sagebrush and rocks without so much as a bump. The horses galloped full speed, hooves kicking up sparks from the ground. Ahead, the reddish desert floor fell away into nothingness.

Frank knew he should pull his head back in the stage, squeeze his eyes shut and not open them until they stopped again, but he became entranced with the approaching cliff, unable to take his eyes off the looming precipice.

Fifty yards away, he found himself wishing for the horses to stop. At thirty, he begged them to turn. At ten, he knew what was going to happen, knew he was helpless to stop it, but he still kept his head out the window, his gaze glued on the point of his impending doom.

Sure enough, the steeds charged right over the edge, plummeting downward with the coach still attached. Frank's stomach lurched, and he fought to not retch as hot desert air washed over his face. Below him, the canyon floor burned, flames leaping from dozens of buildings, all growing larger every second the stagecoach fell.

Frank screamed, and jerked his head back inside just before they hit. Then the world went black.

* * *

The sticky, sharp scent of pine mingled with a hint of perfume in Frank's darkened world, teasing him to open his eyes. But he didn't want to. He wanted to stay in the warm, dark place he'd found, keep smelling pine and perfume, and pretend he didn't have to wake up. A dozen points of pain on his back told him he lay on the pebbly ground, and the warmth on his face told him he faced the sun. The muffled sound of voices reached him from his right—a man and a woman—and birds serenaded him from the trees that whispered in the wind. Somewhere nearby, a dog panted.

He opened one eye, then slammed it shut again as sunlight blinded him, driving spikes of pain into his temples. He threw a forearm across his eyes.

"He's awake," a woman cried, her voice deep and familiar.

They rushed to his side, shadows making the too-bright sunlight flicker and flash.

"Get that blanket!" the man shouted.

The bright sun muted itself, and Frank ventured to open his eyes. A moment later, the dog licked his face, its breath smelling like something not long dead. Frank batted away the cold, wet nose and struggled to sit upright. Hands under his arms helped him, and again, the smell of perfume tickled his nose. Flies buzzed all around him and he raised a sluggish arm to swipe at them.

"Don't be stupid." The woman's voice came from behind him now. "You'll break something off. You've been dead longer than we have, so your body still needs time to rebuild."

He turned his head toward her voice. She was dressed like a man, only her long, blond curls bobbing in the sun identifying her as female. Her gray button shirt and black vest hid any hint of her figure, and under her worn, gray hat, her face seemed plain, unadorned by makeup, though the blue of her eyes rivaled that of the sky behind her. At her side lay a Winchester lever action rifle, and in her belt, she'd tucked a Bowie knife.

Still, she seemed familiar somehow. "Do I know you?"

His eyes adjusted and he noticed a pair of meaty hands holding a rough, gray blanket over their heads.

"Once, long ago," she answered, voice harsh as broken glass. "I'm Camille. We met in a saloon. The night you shot…a horse thief."

Shards of memories raced back to him. Clangy piano music. Pipe smoke and bad whiskey mixing with the smell of the same cheap perfume he smelled now. This woman — dressed in lace and lipstick and finery — sitting on his lap, her face painted so she looked like someone different. He remembered a mole tucked deep down in her ample cleavage but could not see it now with her shirt buttoned to her neck. She'd caught his fancy that night, but events had gotten out of hand.

He'd taken Camille to his room, but before anything could happen, a scrawny half-Indian boy had tried to steal his horse. Frank had put a bullet right between his shoulder blades and left him to die in the street.

Only after his own death, during his time in the underworld, had Frank learned that boy had been his son. He'd committed an unforgivable sin.

"Ron…" He shook the cobwebbed memories from his head.

"Ahem, can I put down this damned blanket now?"

This voice Frank knew the moment he heard it and he confirmed it by looking back at the sausage-like fingers holding the blanket.

Frank's hand drifted toward the reassuring cold steel of the six shooter on his right hip. He wrapped his fingers around the handle, wondering when he'd gotten the pistol back. At his feet lay the lasso, cuffs, and whiskey bottle Buzzy had given him, arranged in a neat pile.

"Now just simmer down," Spike said, lowering the blanket until the sun shone right in Frank's eyes. "I'm here to help you. And you can't go shooting everyone. Not here."

The stout bartender knelt in front of Frank, biceps bulging inside his white shirt, block-shaped head sporting a cautious grin, complete with a missing front tooth. His brown eyes looked almost black compared to Camille's. He held out Frank's old black hat, its satin band frayed, a new crow's feather stuck in the side. Frank took the hat and stuffed it on his head.

"Last time I saw you, you were a giant slug with a horn and a pig snout, pointing a shotgun at me," Frank said. He remembered the run-down saloon in the underworld's version of Tombstone like he'd been there yesterday. "And now you're here to help me?"

Camille's hand found Frank's forearm and her finger paused on the lattice of scars under his sleeve, her short nails tracing along the line. Then, she eased his hand away from his gun.

"We're all here to help you, Frank. Spike, me, and Batcho."

She pointed to the right, where the dog sat, scruffy tail sweeping the desert sand into tiny clouds. No, not a dog, Frank realized...a coyote, with matted brown-and-gray fur, golden eyes, and a collar of beads around his neck. His pink tongue lolled out of his mouth, dripping slobber into the hard-packed earth.

Frank looked at the one-time Indian guide, his mind working. Then, without warning, he started to laugh.

They didn't have a prayer.

CHAPTER FIVE

"**W**hat's that smell?" Frank asked.

He'd first noticed the foul stench just after waking up. Sticky and rotten, the stink had assailed his nostrils like an army of corpses left in the sun too long. Now, after an hour's walk, the smell clung to him like a shroud, drawing flies that swarmed around them no matter what they did.

Batcho sniffed at Frank's hand, whimpered, and trotted ahead to walk closer to Camille.

"What's your problem?" Frank muttered.

All around them, the Rocky Mountains stood grim and silent, gravestones in a giant granite cemetery. The only sounds came from the wind slipping through pine and spruce and the incessant buzzing of the flies. No birds chirped. No squirrels chattered.

Nothing.

"Uh, Marshal," Spike said, "that there ripeness, well, that's you."

Frank stopped and sniffed at his armpit, and sure enough, the stench nearly knocked him over.

"You stink, Frank," Camille said, offering him a crystal bottle of her own perfume, which he waved off. "You were dead for two years and your body still isn't done rebuilding yet."

"Now, don't worry, Marshal—"

"Don't call me that, Spike. I'm no marshal."

The badge burned into the flesh of his chest screamed in pain as if to contradict him.

"All right then, Frank," the bartender said, "don't worry too much. You look fine from a distance, and in a day or two you'll be okay up close, too."

Frank shook his head. "How bad am I? You three look pretty normal to me."

Camille and Spike exchanged a glance, and then both looked at the coyote. Batcho tucked his tail and whined.

Sighing, Frank tugged off his left glove and sucked in his breath. His skin was a deathly pallor, blue veins running under it like underground rivers. He yanked off his other glove to find his right hand—his shooting hand—much more normal.

Camille cleared her throat, and Frank found his companions looking at him, varying degrees of doubt on their faces. He held out his hand to the woman.

"Let me see," he said.

She produced a hand mirror from a pouch at her waist, flipped it open, and handed it to Frank.

It was worse than he'd expected. His skin had rotted through under his left eye, exposing pink flesh and sagging away from the bloodshot eye. The scar running down his cheek lay open, caked with dried blood and pus, and his teeth shone yellow and rotting in the mid-morning sun. He didn't even want to think what the bullet hole in his ribcage probably looked like. The hole that had killed him.

"You were dead much longer than us," said Camille. "There was a lot more damage to repair, so it'll take longer. Be patient. And stand downwind from me."

She winked and gave him the slightest of grins, as if unsure of herself.

Frank handed back her mirror and pulled his gloves back on. At least his tattered, tan duster hid most of him from view. It also hid the lasso and cuffs looped through his belt, and held the holy-whiskey bottle in its pocket.

Spike handed him a bandanna. "In the meantime, Mar…I mean Frank, we probably shouldn't let people see you that way. It would alert the James boy to our coming."

Frank wrapped the bandanna around his face, leaving just his eyes exposed. He'd have to make sure he didn't get close enough for anyone to see.

They started out again, hiking south along a rutted dirt road that meandered down the ravine, a frowning Camille and the coyote in the lead, followed by Frank and then Spike bringing up the rear, shotgun in hand. Several times, the hooker and the coyote stopped, Batcho wanting to go one direction, Camille another. Frank went with Camille's instincts every time. He still didn't trust the former Indian guide.

"Damned coyote is trying to get us lost."

After a few minutes of walking in silence, Spike asked, "What did they offer you?"

"What do you mean?"

"Was it absolution? Less suffering in the pit? They offered me and Camille life."

Frank raised an eyebrow. "That was an option?"

"Not really *life*," Camille clarified. "Even The Boss can't do that. But if we succeed and don't get our bodies killed again, we can stay here as long as we want. Maybe settle old business."

Her blue eyes flashed.

"No more Hell for me," Spike muttered. "No more damned pit of fire, either."

Frank changed the subject. "So, I understand how Camille ended up in Hell. Prostitution's always been a sin. But what about you, Spike? I always thought you a decent man in life."

Camille barked a harsh laugh. "You thinking my job got me sent to Hell?"

But she offered no further explanation, and Spike just looked off into the pines, his gaze distant. "We all have our vices."

They'd gone just a few minutes more when a lone figure rounded a bend ahead of them. His red flannel shirt looked like it hadn't been washed in months, and his ratty gray beard was tangled and matted. The old man slowed when he saw them, tipping back his worn, floppy hat and hitching up his suspenders. He kept a few yards of distance, hefting a pickaxe in his left hand.

"Greetings, stranger!" Spike lifted his hand as he called out, lowering his shotgun to show peaceful intent. "Can you tell us where we are? We appear to be lost."

The old man studied them a moment longer, then shrugged and moved down the hill toward them. A Navy revolver bobbed on his left hip, handle forward, and Frank put his hand on his own pistol. Again, Camille eased it away.

"You're about thirty minutes north of Creede," the man said, drawing near Spike and Camille. Batcho trotted up, scruffy tail pumping back and forth, and sniffed the man's hand. Frank decided to keep his distance. Something seemed off about the old timer. "Or what's left of Creede. It's just through this pass a ways, along the trail."

"What do you mean 'what's left of it?'" Camille asked.

The old man eyed Frank sidelong, his hand twitching near the handle of his gun. The blue of his eyes was crisp, clear, and cold as ice. Frank decided the prospector was probably pretty damn quick on the draw, no matter how long his teeth. There was more to him than met the eye, making Frank fight the urge to put his hand on his own pistol.

The prospector looked at Camille, his eyes narrowing. "Burned damn near down four days ago. Folks all livin' in tents now, hopin' to rebuild before winter sets in."

"What date is it now?" Frank asked.

Again the old man locked eyes with him, sending a chill down his spine.

"June ninth, 1892. Where'd you folks say you were from?"

"We didn't," Frank answered, squaring his shoulders. "You come from Creede?"

The prospector lowered his hand from his pistol and nodded, anxious to move along.

"You notice anyone acting unusual?" Frank asked. "Unusual violence, strength, that kind of thing?"

The prospector shook his head, but the way his eyes opened told Frank that wasn't true.

"You'd better 'fess up." Camille lowered her voice, fingering the handle of her Bowie. Frank let his hand slip to his holster. Finally.

The old man swallowed hard. "Well, maybe Ed O'Kelley. He shot Bob Ford yesterday, out of nowhere.

Just walked into the tent saloon, said 'howdy,' and shot him dead."

Spike and Camille both glanced at Frank. Even the coyote cocked his head to one side.

"Mighty obliged," Frank said.

Without another word, he trudged up the hill, posse in tow. At the top, he turned to find the old man staring after them. Something about him seemed ominous, like a midnight cloud passing in front of the moon. Frank shivered. But then the old timer moved off down the trail and the feeling passed.

The prospector had told them true, and just over the hill they found the trail. They followed it for thirty minutes and came to a kind of doorway to the ravine. Tall peaks rose three or four hundred feet on either side of the canyon, forming an almost fortress-like barrier to the town. The narrow dirt path marked the only way through.

"We'll be lined up like ducks in a barrel going through there," Spike said, straining his neck to stare up at the eastern peak. "Someone could just pick us off."

Frank spit in the dirt. "We're dead already. What do we care?"

"Some of us don't want to go back." Camille muttered. "Got things to do here."

Ignoring her, Frank loosened his pistol in the holster and trudged down the trail.

As soon as they cleared the pass, Creede appeared, making them stop and stare.

Tendrils of smoke still wound their way up from the blackened husks that had once been the business district. Tents dotted the valley—stark and white against the charred remains of the town—like maggots on a corpse.

To their left, a mine tunnel gaped, several miners staring at the strangers.

Entering the town didn't make it any better. People moved sluggishly through the streets, dressed in mourners' black, heads hung, staring at their feet. Some lifted their eyes to glance at the strangers, but most didn't seem to notice, their thoughts gone with the smoke. Only the children seemed unfazed by the smoking ruins of their town, running and playing like it was just another summer day.

Frank peeked under his glove and found his skin less pale, the veins more subtle. He hoped his face was healing faster, too, and tugged the bandanna down around his neck.

When Camille asked, a passerby directed them to the sheriff's office, one of the few buildings still standing. Frank and his group approached the front, where a man lounged in a black suit, a matching hat flat on his head. His mouth hid inside a bushy beard, and a six gun rode at his waist. Something about the man seemed off, shifty.

"You the sheriff?" Frank asked. He moved his hand away from his gun. They weren't here for trouble.

The man rose and flashed an oily smile as he descended the wooden steps, extending a hand.

"Jeff Smith," he said. "Folks call me Soapy. Sheriff Light's left town, so I'm holding things down until the marshal gets here. I'm the sheriff's brother-in-law, and boss of this town."

Anyone who called himself "boss" had to be trouble, and sure enough, the man's handshake was too tight, like he was trying to outdo Frank.

"Understand you have a murderer named O'Kelley locked up," Frank said.

"Red? Yep, he's in there. Damndest thing, him killing Bob. Like he wasn't himself."

"We'd be mighty obliged if we could palaver with

him a moment or two," Spike said. A handful of armed men had gathered behind them, while everyone else fled the street. "We don't want trouble, boss. Just a few questions and we'll move along."

Smith gave them a once over and shook his head. "Not armed, you won't. How do I know you're not old members of the Ford family, come to get even?"

Frank considered their situation, catching Camille's slight head shake and Spike's nervous glance at the men behind them. Batcho trotted over, tongue wagging in the sun, and lifted his leg at the closest thug. The man danced out of the way just before the yellow fluid would have hit his boot.

He turned a bright red and reached for his pistol.

"Steady, Jack," Smith said. "No need for shooting. Yet."

Frank took off his gun belt and handed it to Spike.

"You and her stay here," he said, nodding to Camille. "Me and Batcho will check on O'Kelley."

Spike and Camille gave him dubious looks, but nodded and faced the men. Frank leaned down and whispered in the hooker's ear.

"If they look to come in, let 'em. All they can do is send me back where I came from. Don't give up your chance at staying here for me."

She nodded again.

Frank turned to Smith. "I'm ready."

"The dog stays outside," the town boss said. "Never did trust a mutt."

Batcho stepped forward, teeth bared.

"He's a coyote," Frank said, moving past Smith without waiting for permission. "He does what he wants, and I don't advise trying to stop him. Not if you like your throat."

Smith huffed and stomped up the stairs behind Frank.

The jail was tinier inside than it looked, with just enough room for a wood stove, a desk, and two narrow holding cells. Wanted posters dotted the wall, and a sawed off shotgun stood in one corner.

Sitting on the floor in one cell was Ed O'Kelley. His dark hair sat in a tussled mess on his head, as thin as weeds, and an undergrown handlebar moustache twitched as he watched the strangers approach. His thin frame seemed folded up on itself, and his beady brown eyes studied them.

"Don't look like much, does he?" Smith asked, a cruel grin distorting his mouth.

"That the weapon?" Frank asked, pointing to the shotgun.

"Yep, sure is. He fired both barrels. Damn near beheaded the man who killed Jesse James."

Frank froze. "Ford killed James?"

Smith nodded. "We told him to leave town, but he insisted on re-opening his saloon in a tent after the fire."

"And O'Kelley killed Ford?"

"Yep."

Frank walked to stand before the cell, staring down at O'Kelley. The killer stared back.

"Why'd you do it?"

O'Kelley shrugged. "Felt like it at the time."

Batcho sat on his haunches, tongue lolled to one side, regarding the murderer calmly. That told Frank all he needed to know. He pivoted on his heel and strode for the door, Batcho and Smith close behind.

"He knows you're coming," said O'Kelley as they strode away.

Frank froze, looking back over his shoulder. "What

did you say?"

The murderer shook himself, as if he'd been daydreaming, and looked at Frank with confusion on his face.

"I didn't say anything."

"You said he knows I'm coming. Who?"

O'Kelley shrugged. "I never said that."

Frank moved like lightning, reaching through the bars to grab O'Kelley by the collar and smash his head into the iron bars. The prisoner flinched and let out a pathetic whimper.

"Who?" Frank shouted. "Tell me!"

O'Kelley said nothing, but Smith touched the cold, hard barrel of his pistol to the base Frank's skull.

"Let my prisoner go," he whispered. "Now."

Frank released O'Kelley and Smith lowered his gun. Rising, Frank straightened his shirt and moved to the door, Batcho trailing.

"You at least could have growled at him," Frank mumbled at the coyote.

Batcho whined and tucked his tail.

Outside, Camille and Spike faced the toughs, rifles at the ready, muscles tense. Camille glowered at the men, while Spike looked worried. The gunmen were just as wound, and the whole thing felt like a powder keg ready to blow.

"He's gone." Frank kept his voice low as he strapped his gun belt back on. "O'Kelley's not possessed now. But he killed the man who killed Jesse James, so we're on the right trail."

"I think the problem now is that our trail—correct or not—goes through these gentlemen." Spike fingered his shotgun as he spoke.

Frank looked over the six men before them,

calculating ways to kill them before they killed him. All other onlookers had gone, leaving just the gunmen with their six shooters and scowls. In the distance, a train whistle blew.

"You'll all want to be on that train," Smith said, coming up behind them. "It leaves town in an hour."

Out the corner of his eye, Frank saw movement in a nearby building. A tiny, freckled face disappeared, replaced by a still-swinging white curtain.

"We're not quite finished yet," he growled at Smith, his hand hovering near his Colt. "I'd like to get a look at the scene of the killing, maybe talk to some—"

"That won't be possible," Smith said, stepping closer. "Tent saloon's torn down, and the witnesses were all interviewed. They had nothing interesting to say."

Frank started to protest, but Smith cut him off. "The train, friends. Now."

CHAPTER SIX

Ten minutes later, Frank and his crew stood amidst a swarm of flies in front of the Creede depot, tickets in-hand. Smith's men had positioned themselves around the area, and a small crowd milled around on the platform, waiting to board a train consisting of three passenger cars, two boxcars, and a caboose.

"So, where do we go now?" Spike asked.

"I say we just get to Alamosa and figure things out from there," replied Camille. Her face was dusty now, giving her a hardened kind of beauty, like she was part of the land. Frank caught himself staring at her and looked away.

At that moment, Batcho went rigid and growled at the far end of the platform. An instant later, the coyote calmed himself and sat, panting in the heat.

"You might be the dumbest coyote ever." Frank turned to the others. "Unless Spike has an objection, we'll head to, uh…"

He realized he didn't know where.

"Minnesota," came a small voice behind him. "Northfield, Minnesota."

Frank turned and looked down at a scrawny boy, nine or ten years old. Soot marred his cheeks and forehead, but Frank recognized his freckles.

"You were watching us earlier, in the window." One of Smith's men took notice, so the boy held out his hand, winking. Frank dug a penny from his pocket and gave it to the boy. The gunman relaxed.

"What are you talking about, son?" Frank asked.

The boy bit down on the penny, then slipped it in his pocket.

"The one you're looking for," the boy answered. "He said he was going to Northfield."

Camille squatted in front of the boy, putting a hand on his shoulder. "If you tell us more, there'll be more money."

For emphasis, she jingled the purse at her waist.

The boy shook his head. "This information costs more than coins."

"You can tell us or it'll be unpleasant for you," Frank grumbled.

This time the boy laughed out loud. "All I gotta do is yell out and those men with the guns will come down on you hot as bacon sizzling."

"You don't know anything," Spike said. "Go on, get lost now before I kick your—"

"He's not alone anymore." Suddenly, the boy had Frank's complete attention. "I know who he's with, what they look like, and what they're up to. Overheard it all."

He crossed his scrawny arms and turned his back on Camille.

"You got grit," Frank told him. "What's your askin' price, then?"

The boy spun, a smile curving up the corners of his impish mouth. "Take me with you."

"No chance."

"That's the price for everything I know about the new James gang. At least, that's what they're calling themselves."

Frank knew the boy was baiting him, but it still worked — he was interested.

Camille stood and turned to Frank. "This is no trip for a child. He'll slow us down or get himself killed."

"It's a chance we gotta take," Frank replied. "We need this information. Bad."

Spike started to object, but Frank cut him off and turned to the boy.

"What's your name, boy?"

"Curtis. Curtis Sheets, sir." He rubbed a soot-covered finger under his nose, leaving a smear.

"And what would your mom and dad say about you going with us?"

Curtis shrugged. "Nothing. They died a few years back and left me to my uncle. He sold me to the mining company to work in the shafts."

"How old are you?"

"Nine. I'm small for my age, but I fit better in the shafts that way. Makes me more useful."

Batcho nudged his head under Curtis's hand and let the boy scratch his ears.

Camille fingered the handle of her Bowie. "I'd like to have a word or two with this uncle of yours."

"Can't," Curtis said. "Got a telegram last year sayin'

he died in a gunfight in Missouri. I got no one here."

Frank looked at both Camille and Spike. Neither objected.

"Looks like we're your best hope, then," Frank said. "But you do what I say and you stay out of the way. This is dangerous business, not child's play."

Curtis puffed out his chest. "I know how dangerous he is. I saw him. When no one else could."

Steam hissed from the locomotive and the conductor bellowed for boarding.

"Go get yourself a ticket to Denver," Frank said, offering Curtis a silver dollar.

But the boy stared over Frank's shoulder, eyes wide and jaw hanging open. Beside him, Batcho growled.

Frank turned. People scattered from the platform, either boarding the train or hurrying into the depot building. Stomping up the stairs and onto the wood planks of the platform was the old prospector. He'd straightened his bent frame now, standing over six feet tall, the pickaxe dragging in his left hand. In his right hand gleamed the Navy revolver, but as bright as it shone, nothing could draw Frank's gaze from the midnight black of the old man's eyes. They bore into him, slicing through him, making him feel exposed and alone. Part of him recoiled, but another jumped at the chance of a fight, something he understood.

Frank drew his pistol. "About time we got to the shootin' part. Spread out!"

Spike and Camille fanned out to either side, and Frank shoved Curtis behind him

The old man fired first, the round whizzing past Frank's ear. His second shot took Frank in the left shoulder with a hollow whump sound but no pain, just the feeling of being punched in the shoulder.

Frank returned fire, his shot tearing through the prospector's chest and exploding out the back in a shower of flesh and bone. The old man didn't slow, instead firing again. This shot ricocheted off the engine, and the fourth struck Frank in the thigh. This time, pain exploded in his leg and up into his hip, nearly making him fall.

Spike finally brought the shotgun to bear and fired both barrels, rocking the prospector backward, tearing off his left arm and sending the pickaxe flying. The damage didn't last, though, as the severed arm reattached itself in a heartbeat, bone and sinew weaving together of its own accord. The old man took aim at the barkeep, and Frank used the moment's distraction to push Curtis toward the railcar.

"Get on the train, boy! Now!"

The boy did as he was told, disappearing into the passenger car.

Camille had joined the fight now, opening fire from behind a post. At least two of her rounds struck the prospector, one knocking him sideways, almost making him fall. The old man let out a wail of fury so loud Frank felt it in his chest, as if someone had stuck him with a sandbag. The prospector turned his pistol toward Camille.

Even as Frank raised his Colt, he knew he was too late. Time seemed to slow, the old man's gun coming up inexorably, Frank's own motions slowed like he was stuck in a vat of molasses. He couldn't make it in time.

The prospector fired again and everything returned to normal, Frank's run picking up steam, even as the train pulled away from the platform. The first shot pinged off the light post where Camille hid, and before the prospector could fire another shot, Frank drove his shoulder into the old man's ribs. They tumbled to the planks, Frank rolling away as the prospector slid on his side the other direction.

Frank came to his feet, gun drawn, and fired one shot, hitting the old man in the center of his chest. Flesh spattered the train car behind him as the prospector teetered on the edge of the platform, then fell between it and the moving train.

For a solitary, still moment, everyone froze, holding their breath as if letting it out would breathe life back into the old man.

"Hurry!" Curtis yelled from inside the first boxcar. "Get on before it leaves!"

Camille moved first, Spike following, both running for the open door.

Batcho yipped and jumped onto the car, slipping past the boy. Camille was just grabbing the rail to pull herself on when movement caught Frank's eye. A hand grasped the edge of the platform, and the prospector hauled himself onto the planks.

"Go!" Frank yelled to the others. He ran, watching as Camille climbed aboard. Spike struggled, being hefty and slow. The big barkeep huffed, arm extended in a futile effort to grab the moving handle.

Frank's leg screamed in pain, but he managed to get close enough to shove Spike in the back, giving the man just enough of a boost to stumble onto the car.

Frank's fingers brushed the cool brass handle as the end of the platform neared. He had just enough space—

A shot rang out and fire stabbed him between the shoulder blades. He stiffened, stumbled, and fell from the end of the platform. He took the three-foot drop hard, smashing into the baked earth, his breath exploding from his chest. He lay stunned for a heartbeat, then he was up and running, pulling air back into his lungs with all his might.

The prospector followed on his heels, fetid breath hot on Frank's neck. Frank's leg slowed him down some, but he still managed to reach the door of an empty box car and grab the hand rail. He was about to lever himself into the car when the prospector dove and grabbed his right ankle, making him stumble.

Frank clung to the rail with one hand while the train built speed, his left foot dragging on the ballast. The prospector began to climb up his leg, reaching his knee in one lunge. His midnight eyes drove railroad spikes of terror into Frank's heart. He kicked at the old man, but he held on with hands of iron.

Frank tried to draw his pistol with his left hand, but couldn't reach. The prospector lunged again, his arms now around Frank's thigh, his mouth bent into a savage grin. The old man drew his pistol, holding onto Frank with one arm, and pushed it into the existing wound. Frank screamed and almost lost his grip on the rail.

"So long, gun fighter," the prospector wheezed. "Jesse sends his regards."

Something streaked over Frank's head, and a pickaxe impaled itself through the prospector's eye, rocking his head back. Curtis grabbed Frank's wrist and held on while Batcho leaned out, his forepaws on Frank's chest, and clamped his jaws down on the old man's wrist. The prospector lost his grip on Frank's leg. With a scream, he rolled under the box car behind them and disappeared.

Curtis and Batcho managed to tug Frank inside, and the three lay on the cold floor, chests heaving. Batcho's tongue flicked in and out of his mouth, spitting out chunks of dead flesh.

Frank reached out to scratch the coyote's ears. "Looks like you ain't so useless."

Batcho bared his teeth in response.

As they watched, the bits of prospector meat coalesced into one larger chunk and crawled out the door. Frank and Curtis exchanged a look, and ran to the door, both peering out behind the train. There, a half-mile back, stood the prospector, watching them go with his dead, black eyes.

"Something tells me we'll be seeing him again," Curtis said.

Frank grunted assent and turned away.

"Thanks for saving my hide," he muttered. "Now let's find the other two and figure this out."

Curtis pointed at Frank's leg. "We'd better take care of that, too."

Frank winced as the pain returned, but shrugged it off. "I'm already dead. What harm's a little hole gonna do?"

CHAPTER SEVEN

Frank rested his head against the supple leather cover of his seat's cushion, closed his eyes. He tried to ignore the sharp pangs of pain in his thigh while Camille cleaned his wound with a foul-smelling brown whiskey they'd bought from a fellow passenger. Frank hadn't offered the whiskey Buzzy had given him—he didn't think it would have the same effect.

"Amazing," she muttered, looking up for a moment, her cold, blue eyes avoiding his. "The wound is healing itself so fast the bullet fell out. If all our bodies do this, we might have a chance at surviving."

He could feel his flesh mending, weaving fibers together as if it had a life of its own.

Outside the window, the gray and brown hues of the Rockies streaked past, a blur of drab earth tones with splotches of green here and there for variety. The sun set behind them, distorting shadows, melting the purple and black of the sky into the surrounding countryside. Inside the train, a solitary fly buzzed, the rest of the swarm left behind.

"Makes sense if you think about it," Spike said, watching her work, wincing with every move as if she were working on his leg. "Our souls brought our bodies back from the dead and healed years of decay. Bullet wounds are light work."

The barkeep sat across from Frank in their private compartment, with Curtis beside him, trying not to look at the blood. At their feet lay Batcho, seemingly asleep, though the occasional twitch of his ear hinted he was aware of more than he let on.

Once she'd cleaned his wound, Camille handed Frank the needle and thread.

"I ain't your seamstress," she said. "Mend your own damned pants."

For an instant, he saw something dark dancing behind the ice of her eyes, something shadowed and frightening. Then she smiled, locking eyes with him, and sat on the bench, leaving a fist's width between them.

He thought for just an instant it had been more than just a smile, like she'd saved it just for him. But that was silly, so he shook it off and looked at Curtis.

"Tell us everything you saw."

Curtis drew in a deep, dramatic breath, and looked at the ceiling.

"I was outside the jail when they brought Red in. Took two men just to get him into the cell. He was yelling, and thrashing, making the biggest fuss when they dragged him in that front door. Marshal Rossen and Sheriff Plunkett did the arresting, and they said he had super-human strength, like he was four men wrapped into one body."

He leaned in close then, as if about to enlighten them with a great secret. He lowered his voice to a hoarse whisper.

"Minute he got inside that cell, they say he went limp, and passed clean out."

"That's when the spirit must have left him," said Camille. She avoided Frank's gaze, now. "Do you know who the spirit possessed next?"

"Sure do!" he nodded as he spoke. "Jeb Fisher. I watched it happen, seein' that he was standing right beside me. One minute he was watching Sheriff Plunkett, the next his eyes turned all black and he smiled all icy and cold. Then, he just turned and walked away without even a word.

"I knew something wasn't right though—I'm a smart boy, they say—so I followed him. Followed him all the way to the Commodore mine, where he hitched up with some no-goods from out of town. They didn't see me listenin' under the foreman's window, but I heard 'em clear as day say they were going to Northfield, Minnesota."

"Did they say what they were going to do there?" Spike asked. "Doesn't seem like a very big place, and if I recall, Jesse likes to make a big show of things, likes to politicize them as the north oppressing southerners."

"They all laughed and griped about making something right, like Jesse had unfinished business."

Frank wracked his brain, trying to recall if the James gang had done anything in Northfield, but he'd never really followed them. He'd had his own problems to look after when he'd been alive.

"Who were these no-goods?" Camille pressed the

boy. "And how many were there?"

"I counted four," Curtis answered. "Mostly small-timers, thugs who worked for Soapy Smith, but crossed him somehow."

"They any good with their guns?" Frank asked.

Curtis nodded. "Most of them are former rebel soldiers. They took a whole wagon load of dynamite, too."

"What about your friend, Mr. Fisher? Can he shoot?"

Curtis opened his mouth to reply, but Camille cut him off.

"Doesn't matter," she said, frowning. "He'll have Jesse's shooting skills."

"So, it's five on three," Frank said. "Good odds."

"Unless our gold-digging friend shows up," Spike added. "We barely handled him last time all by himself."

"And they said they were hoping to meet someone with your same name in Northfield," Curtis tossed out. "Frank."

"Jesse has a brother named Frank." Spike said, yawning. "They made a deadly team."

Taking on the James brothers wouldn't give Frank's posse as good a chance. They were seasoned soldiers, guerrilla fighters who'd massacred dozens of Union soldiers without so much as blinking an eye. But if he had to face them, at least Minnesota was out of their stomping grounds, away from the hordes of sympathizers who worshipped them like heroes. People from Arkansas through Texas and into Missouri saw the James brothers as folk legends, robbing the rich to give to the poor. Except they never seemed to get to the giving part.

"We need to get there quick, then," Frank said. "Our escaped prisoner is up to something."

The door to their compartment slid open and a dapper-looking man in a suit and bowler, a thick moustache on his lip, and a shield-shaped badge on his chest stepped inside their compartment.

"Did I hear something about escaped prisoners?"

His voice reminded Frank of silk, smooth and cool on the ear.

"Just small talk," he answered. "Nothing serious enough for a mighty Pinkerton man to worry about."

The detective helped himself to the bench on the other side of Camille, making the one-time hooker slide closer to Frank until their thighs touched and her hand drifted toward her knife. He looked the group over one by one, swatting at the fly that buzzed around his head.

"You're a might heavily armed for run-o-the-mill travelers," he quipped, moustache jerking up and down. "You folks wouldn't be a posse crossing county lines, would you?"

"We're no posse," Frank lied. "Just on our way to Minnesota and heard travel could be dangerous through the mountains."

The detective looked unconvinced.

"Who ever heard of a posse with children?" Curtis interjected, smiling a rogue's charming smile. "My ma and pa here just want to get us to our new home safe-like. They even told me, they said, 'if only the brave men of the Pinkerton Agency were here to protect us, we wouldn't need these weapons.'"

The detective gave the boy a long, hard stare, then shook his head and stood.

"You folks stay out of trouble now, hear?"

He left the compartment, sliding the door closed behind him.

"Go back to roughing up miners," Curtis grumbled after him.

After a moment, Spike looked at Frank.

"I may know how to slow down our prospector friend. Did they give you Holy Water?"

"Kind of." Frank removed the whiskey bottle from his duster pocket and started to hand it to Spike. He paused, then extended it to Curtis instead.

"Take a little drink," he ordered. "Let's make sure you're alive."

Curtis looked at Camille, who shrugged.

"Do it, if you know what's good for you."

Curtis grinned and popped the cork. Everyone stared at him as he took a tiny swig of the whiskey and choked.

"Yuck," he said, sticking out his tongue, "it tastes so...old."

When nothing happened to him, Frank breathed a sigh of relief and handed the bottle back to Spike.

"Now give me your bullets," said the stout barkeep. "And a candle."

An hour later, using a tin cup and a knife, he'd hollowed all the bullet points, filled them with drops of Holy-whiskey, and sealed them with wax. Then he dipped each one in Holy-whiskey and reloaded them into the guns or ammo belts, leaving just a few shot glasses-worth in the bottle. Camille handed him her Bowie knife and he coated that in the stuff, as well.

"That might not kill the prospector," he said, "but it ought to slow him down a bit."

"What was that thing back there?" Curtis asked.

"Not exactly sure," Frank told him. "But Buzzy warned me James might bring someone else back to help him, and it looks like he did. Whoever he brought borrowed that old prospector's body.

"Don't matter though. Soon as we get to Denver, we're dropping you off with a foster home, so you'll never see that old man again."

If Frank hadn't seen the little con artist in action, he might have believed the look of indignation on his face, and fallen for the crossed arms.

"That's not fair," Curtis pouted. "You promised to take me with you, not dump me like an unneeded burden..."

"We never said how far—"

"...just like my uncle did!"

Tears welled in the boy's eyes, glistening like flakes of silver—or in this case, fool's silver, if there was such a thing. Spike looked ready to brim over, too, but Camille wasn't fooled, crossing her own arms across her chest and glaring at the boy. Frank grunted and tried to keep a grin from spreading across his face. He failed.

Curtis realized his trick wasn't working and changed tactics, dropping his arms and looking Frank in the eye.

"Besides," he said, "I'm the only who knows what Jeb looks like. And I can see the dead people walking before most folks, like I spotted that prospector-thing before you did. You need me."

Camille's expression didn't change, but Spike nodded.

"He's right, Frank."

Frank fought down a groan, but relented with a nod. "So, how do you see them, anyway?"

The boy shrugged. "Dunno. I just see this shimmering glow around them, like they're shining. Saw it the minute one moved into Jeb's body. Been seeing it all my life. Used to scare me, but not anymore."

"Do you see it around all of us?"

He seemed to study Frank for a moment, squinting his eyes. "It's different around you. Barely visible. More like a shadow than a shine. Makes me shiver, honestly."

"Adds up," Spike told them. "We're all using our old,

dead bodies. Jesse's using living ones. Interaction between life and death is bound to be a little different."

That made Frank's head hurt, so he changed the subject.

"How much dynamite did you say the gang took with 'em?"

"A whole buckboard full," Curtis said, settling back in his seat with a satisfied smile. "I counted six crates."

"What are you thinking, Frank?" asked Camille. She still hadn't moved away from him, and he tried not to think about the firm brush of her fingers against his thigh. Dead or not, she stirred something in him. He cleared his throat.

"Seems a bit much for a simple bank robbery, don't you think?"

"Agreed," she said, finally sliding away from him, breaking contact with his leg. He missed it instantly. "Shouldn't need more than one crate to blow a vault, less if you're going in through a side wall."

Frank scratched the stubble on his chin. It hadn't grown a bit since he'd woken up outside Creede.

"Looks like the new James gang is robbing something big," he said. "Question is, what?"

CHAPTER EIGHT

Trains didn't run direct between Creede and Northfield, or as far as Frank could tell, between Creede and just about anywhere. So his group changed trains in Alamosa, Denver, and again in Minneapolis, all the while looking over their shoulders for the prospector.

They ran into no trouble, even when forced to spend a night in a hotel in Denver, just outside the depot. But even in their cramped, smoke-stained hotel room, the ever-needed vigilance chased sleep away. Spike polished his shotgun, Camille sharpened her knife for hours, and Frank paced, anxious to be on their way again.

So, when their train pulled up next to the small, brick station in Northfield at noon two days later, his group looked like they were slowly returning to the world of the dead. Camille had developed streaks of blue around her lips, while the flesh on Spike's neck had rotted and started to slough off, requiring the big barkeep to cover his neck with a kerchief despite the baking heat and smothering humidity. Frank could smell his own flesh rotting again, and he didn't dare look under his sleeves for fear of exposing the damage there. He had his own personal cloud of flies buzzing around him again, too, driving people away.

Only Curtis and the coyote seemed unblemished, but neither had struggled with sleep as the others had.

As they disembarked, Frank pulled them aside, away from the crowd, beside the scorching hot surface of the depot's bricks.

"We need someplace safe to hole up and get some sleep. Apparently dead bodies don't do well without some resting in peace."

The others nodded in silence, too tired to expend the energy to speak.

"I'll find us a place," Curtis promised, and he disappeared into the milling throng of people without waiting for permission.

They found a wooden bench in the shade of the depot's north side and sat, sluggish and despondent, Batcho flopped out in the dirt at their feet. Frank paid for a newspaper from a passing boy and checked the date.

"July twelfth, 1892." He handed the paper to Camille. "See if you can find any clues in here about what our escaped spirit could be up to here in Northfield."

Camille nodded, but a moment later, Curtis returned, beaming.

"I found us a place. It's in a great spot and cheap. And I think I know why Jesse James is here."

They stood to follow him, but Batcho froze, his hackles rising and his lips peeling back in a low, guttural growl. The coyote stared at the train platform, and as Frank followed his gaze, the feeling of being watched crept across his skin, like a snake brushing against him. No, not just watched—hunted.

The moment passed, Batcho relaxed, and Frank's stomach un-knotted. He sighed and followed the boy. Curtis led them out of the depot and down a wide dirt road to an iron bridge. Still on foot, they crossed the bridge, dodging wagons and riders on horseback, the river making a smooth, rushing sound under their feet. Frank hurried across—his last experience with rivers had been in the underworld, and had been unpleasant. Once on the other side, they found themselves in a large square, looking north at a stone two-story building with arched windows on both levels. The left side bore a sign saying, "Lee & Hitchcock," while the right sign read, "W. Scriver."

"Remember that building," Curtis said. Then he hurried down the street in front of it, slipping to the side of a three-story brick building with canvas awnings and a sign reading, "Dampier House" out front. A stooped old man with milky blue eyes and hair the color of snow waited at the bottom of a set of iron stairs leading to the second floor.

"Give him a dollar," Curtis told Frank. "He has a room for us on the second floor with a fire escape out the back door."

"Thought you said this was cheap," Frank complained as he fished a silver dollar from his inside pocket. The old man snatched it from his hand lightning fast, then stood aside so Curtis could lead them up the stairs.

Their room had a bed large enough for two adults, and a sofa big enough for a third.

"I'll take first watch," Frank offered. "You three get

some sleep, so Spike and Camille's bodies can repair themselves."

"Don't you wanna know why he's here?" Curtis begged.

"Of course we do," Camille told him, stretching out on the couch with a gaping yawn. "Just be quick before we fall asleep."

The boy perked up, his face glowing with pride. He paced the room, making quite the presentation.

"That building I told you to remember?" They all nodded sleepily. "Well, on the right side of it—across Division Street from our room — is the First National Bank of Northfield, the bank the James-Younger gang tried to rob in 1876. Tried and failed."

Frank leaned out their only window and studied the front of the bank. Nothing unusual caught his eye.

"I remember now," said Spike. "Locals fought back. Killed a couple of the gang members and stopped the robbery."

Curtis beamed as he nodded. "Looks like he's tying up loose ends in the living world."

Frank nodded, but something didn't feel right, like he was seeing just one or two trees in a vast forest. As the boy lay down beside Spike and Batcho curled up on the floor, Frank gazed out the window. Across the street, a shadow shifted in front of the Scriver building, little more than a shimmer in the hot summer air, but for an instant, Frank thought it took on the shape of some massive beast, a shimmering waver of light with glowing yellow eyes that sent a chill down his spine. His right hand strayed to his pistol, while the left clasped around the steel cuffs.

He shook himself, and the feeling passed. Nearby, Camille started to snore.

Sometime later—with the sun dipping into the

orange and red colors of its evening paint palette—she joined him at the window, leaning against the opposite frame and staring into the street in silence. The crowd had thinned, and even though he'd watched non-stop, the shimmer had not reappeared. During his time in the underworld, he'd learned that such shimmers happened when the denizens of the underworld ventured too close to the world of the living. Not a good sign, he decided.

Still, the unmistakable feeling of being watched clung to him like fog to a gravestone.

After a few minutes, Camille brushed her finger across the scar on his cheek.

"You need sleep." Her half-whisper was throaty and soft. "Your body needs to rebuild."

"Do I smell that bad?"

"Worse," she replied. "Your stench woke me up and I think it's giving the coyote nightmares."

On the floor, Batcho twitched and yipped like he was chasing rabbits. Or prospectors.

Frank looked at her, and this time she met his gaze.

"So, if it wasn't your…job, what landed you in Hell?"

She straightened and her hand dropped to the knife riding her hip. She gazed out the window into the darkness beyond the glass.

Her words came like icicles dropping on stones. "I stabbed a…client."

Frank thought about that. "Doesn't seem like sticking a John would be quite enough to earn your soul's eternal damnation."

"Two."

Frank raised an eyebrow. "Two?"

"I stabbed two Johns. And a Steve. Pair of Bobs. At least three Mikes. I left a trail of dead solicitors from San Fran to Saint Louis before one finally got the knife out of my hands and turned it on me. Twenty-four kills. Probably more than you."

She stole a look in his direction, and Frank made sure to hide his shock at her confession. So much made sense now—her dislike of men, the knife, even her sour demeanor.

"Twenty-seven," he mumbled. "I got you by three."

She stared at him a moment longer, then looked out the window again.

"They deserved it," she said, her voice distant. "Everyone of 'em hurt me. Paying for my body like it was a horse."

"So, that night you and I met..."

He let it dangle there between them.

"I would have killed you, too. You'd have been number thirteen, but then you...well, you know."

She looked at the floor.

"Well, I'd take you stabbing me over me shooting my son," he told her, looking out into the darkened street. "Maybe then I could..."

Her fingers lighted on his shoulder, skating down the back of his arm and lingering on his elbow. She turned him to face her, looking up into his eyes, lips parted. The handle of the Bowie dug into his hip as she pressed herself against him.

"I don't much want to stab you now. I'd rather—"

"We're both dead," he said, cutting her off.

"Exactly," she breathed. "We're both condemned to Hell already, so what more can they do to us?"

Frank took in the scent of her hair, a mix of lilac and powder, and felt himself stirring inside. It would have been easy to let her have her way, to give her what she wanted. Or at least he thought it would. After all, she was right. What more could the judges do?

That was the problem with losing restraints, he thought. Without consequences, knowing right from wrong didn't matter, most people would still choose wrong. Her lips brushed his, and for a moment he almost gave in. But something in his gut screamed at him, warning him this was wrong. Unnatural.

Putting both hands on her shoulders, he eased her back.

"And when this is over," he said, "I'll go back to Hell where I belong, but you'll remain here."

She looked away, turning her back to him and crossing her arms over her chest.

"He knew we were coming," he muttered. She turned back around, head cocked to one side. "O'Kelley slipped into a kind of trance and told me James knows we're coming for him."

She shrugged. "Lucky guess. He had to know the judges would send someone."

"I don't think so. I think he knew who was coming and where we'd come from. The prospector met us in that pass, after all."

"Why didn't he kill us there?" she asked, sliding close and leaning her shoulder on his chest. "Would've caught us with our petticoats up around our bellybuttons."

Frank pondered that, but couldn't come up with anything that made sense.

"Maybe he wasn't ready or needed time to gain more power. Or maybe, at that point, he was still just an old man. But I know one thing, damn straight."

"What's that?"

"Someone tipped him off," Frank answered, returning his gaze to the street. "Hell has a mole."

CHAPTER NINE

The sun sliced through the thick morning air like a golden knife blade, carving the street outside into slices of dark and light. Frank had slept only a little, returning to the window an hour or so before dawn, but his body felt restored a bit. Certainly not alive, not in the truest sense of the word, but well enough to attack their morning tasks with some vigor.

The old man with the milky eyes brought them a breakfast of eggs and bacon, with cold milk to wash it down. Curtis attacked the food like a ravenous wolf, keeping watch out the window while his friends exchanged confused glances.

"You sure we can't eat?" Spike asked, licking his lips.

Frank had to admit, the crisp smell of bacon taunted him, as if it knew a man in Hell felt hungry every minute of every day.

"I'm sure," Frank said. "Buzzy was very specific."

Curtis choked on a piece of bacon, spitting the fatty meat out the window and pointing, holding his throat with the other hand. The three rushed to his side, Spike thumping him between the shoulder blades.

"That's one of 'em," the boy choked. "One of the new James gang. The man in the black vest."

Frank should have noticed the man right away, with his confident swagger, darting eyes, and one hand always poised near the pistol on his hip. He'd faced many men like him in life, killed most.

The man strolled across the dusty street, trying too hard to look casual, but glanced at the Scriver building with the regularity of a Swiss watch. He climbed the steps to the front door of a drug store down the street from the hotel and stepped inside, flashing one last too-cautious glance at the bank as he went.

"I know a casing when I see one," Spike said. "Men like that used to stake out my bar in Tombstone, trying to figure if I was worth robbing."

"You weren't," Frank said. Spike looked hurt for a moment, then shrugged.

A few minutes later, the man left the store and strolled north across the square, still trying to look nonchalant while he studied the Scriver building. Then he turned right and disappeared.

"West on Fourth Street," Spike said.

Frank looked at Curtis. "Is he…dead, like us?"

The boy shook his head.

"Okay, then let's see where he's going." Frank loosened his pistol in its holster and started for the door before Camille stopped him with a hand on his elbow.

"Find out where he goes, then meet me back here."

"Where are you going?" he asked.

She pulled her purse from her belt and jingled the coins inside. "Shopping. A girl can't exactly flirt with a man while she's dressed like one."

"I know what you're thinking," Frank grumbled, but she didn't let him finish.

"Then you know I'm right. This is the best way to find out what's going on. Spike, I could use a man to carry things, and I suspect Frank needs our young friend's special vision."

She wheeled and marched out, leaning her rifle against the wall. The barkeep gave Frank a helpless expression and followed her, lugging his shotgun.

"Watch her back," Frank told him.

"She can watch mine," he replied as he left.

Frank told Batcho to stay in the room, not needing the attention a coyote would draw, and left with Curtis in tow.

By the time Frank and Curtis found the man again, he was a good hundred yards down Fourth Street, moving like he had somewhere to be. Frank pretended to shop with Curtis, pausing to look in store windows periodically. Curtis played his part well, pointing and smiling a lot, but saying nothing.

Finally, the gang member stopped in front of a ramshackle two-story, glanced around, and slipped inside. Frank read the sign over the door, then set a brisk pace back to the hotel, Curtis jogging to keep up.

* * *

Just before noon, Camille and Spike returned, Spike looking exhausted and Camille looking like she had the first time Frank met her. She wore a striking blue dress that made her eyes shine so bright they eclipsed the summer sky outside their window. Her ample cleavage gleamed, and her golden curls bounced like the sun had poured itself in liquid form over her head and shoulders.

"So," she said, her voice bawdy and inviting now, its harshness gone, "where's a girl gotta go to find some action in this town?"

Frank suppressed a chuckle and looked her over from top to bottom. She twirled for him, her dress lifting enough to show off her black fishnet stockings. He caught a whiff of sticky-sweet perfume.

"You look darn nice," Frank said. "For a dead woman."

She slugged him and turned away.

"Remember, gunfighter, I still have the knife under all this finery."

Frank looked at Spike, but the bartender glanced at the ceiling. Curtis had moved to the window, but stood, shaking his head at Frank.

"Ah, just keep an eye on that bank," Frank grumbled.

"So, where am I going?" Camille said. "I want to get out of this ridiculous dress."

Frank grunted. "Place called The Exchange. Supposed to look like an eatery, but it's a saloon."

She nodded and stomped out, her dress swishing behind her.

Frank looked at Curtis. "Follow her. Stay outta sight, but come get me if she needs help."

The boy gave a curt nod and ran from the room.

"Boy's got grit," Spike muttered. "I'll give him that much."

"Hope it don't get him killed."

Spike paused a moment, fumbling with words.

"Come out and ask it," Frank said, "whatever it is. I won't get mad."

Spike looked away, the corners of his eyes wrinkling. "You got a thing for Camille?"

Frank studied the thick bartender. "Why? You got eyes for her?"

Spike nudged at the rug with the toe of his boot.

"No, but I tend to...well, I have a weakness for women-folk. Especially ones that are spoken for. It's gotten me in some trouble."

Frank laughed and clapped his old friend on the shoulder.

"So the ninth commandment sent you to Hell, eh?" Spike nodded, making Frank chuckle again. "Well, don't fret. She was a hooker in life. Only men speakin' for her were the ones on paper money."

Spike didn't seem comforted, and Frank wondered if he'd seen something between them.

The next two hours crawled by like snails on a hot street. The bank was quiet, occasional customers entering or leaving, but none even a little suspicious. Neither Camille nor Curtis showed up, and eventually, Frank's patience wore out.

"Let's go," he told Spike.

They positioned themselves outside the hidden saloon, Frank leaning against a pole in front of a drug store, smoking a cigar he'd bought inside. Spike made small talk with a woman across the street—a married one, of course—both men keeping one eye on the saloon.

Frank was so focused on the door that he jumped when an older boy—maybe twelve or thirteen, with pistols on each hip—marched up the steps and shoved into the store, tossing the door aside like it offended him. The boy carried himself with an arrogance uncommon in one so young, and it made Frank's skin tingle. As soon as he entered The Exchange, the feeling passed and Frank shook himself.

"Now my mind's playing games with me."

That mindset lasted about a minute, until Curtis sprinted out of an alley beside the saloon, skidding to a stop in front of Frank. Spike heaved himself across the street to join them.

"They're gone," Curtis spouted, his words tumbling out, tripping on one another. "The whole gang just slipped out the back door, mounted up, and headed west."

"Camille?" Frank asked.

"Took her with 'em. She looked right at me, Frank, but her eyes were all blank, like she didn't see me."

"The bank," Spike muttered.

Without hesitation, they sprinted back the way they'd come.

CHAPTER TEN

Frank burst into Bridge Square as the first shots split the muggy afternoon air and the sound of horses thundered through the street. A group of men on horseback galloped around the square in front of the bank, firing pistols at the sky and shouting the old rebel yell. Spike slid to a stop beside him, with Curtis panting up behind.

Bystanders were scattering like mice before a cat, ducking for cover or locking themselves inside.

"Get under cover," Frank told them both, loosening his Colt in the holster. "Use the Winchester and cover me. Time to end this little square dance."

Spike took off at a run, but the boy remained, staring up at Frank.

"Go on, son!" Frank yelled. "You're not dead yet, so let's try to keep it that way." A bullet whizzed past his ear as if to drive home his point.

"I can help! Just watch me!"

Before Frank could protest, the boy ran off down a side street and out of sight.

"Frank Butcher!" The voice sounded high-pitched and reedy, but that was just the thin layer of ice over a frigid river of power that lurked underneath. Frank turned and found himself looking up at a boy on horseback, the same boy he'd seen at the saloon. Only this time, his eyes were black as death and he pointed his revolvers at Frank.

"Jeb Fisher, I presume?" Frank fingered the lasso under his duster, knowing he was nowhere close enough to use it. His heart climbed into his throat.

The boy's laugh slithered through the now-empty street like a sidewinder.

"Jeb's all tied up right now, so you'll have to deal with me."

"Jesse James," Frank spat, as two more gang members rode up beside the boy, guns still smoking as they reloaded. "And I suppose you know why I'm here, too."

"Might as well let me see it," Jesse James ordered. "Show me the badge you think gives you authority to take me back."

Frank peeled back his shirt to show the pink, swollen badge the judges had branded on him. It seemed to react to the presence of the spirit, glowing a dark blue, like steel under his skin.

"That's real pretty," said the soul of Jesse James, holstering his guns. "But it don't mean squat to me, and it shouldn't to you, either."

James and his men dismounted, the leader handing his reins to one of his men. He strode up the steps to the hotel porch, two cronies flanking him.

"How ya figure?" Frank asked, keeping the men in front of him.

Jeb-Jesse grinned, a slick, oily expression that seeped onto his face. "Because you know as well as I do those judges are lying. They want something, and you're just a tool to help them get it. What'd they promise you? Relief from the eternal agony of Hell?"

"Nope," Frank said. His hand hesitated near the handle of his Colt. Curtis had neglected to mention that Jeb Fisher was just a boy. "But my demands ain't your business. You can come along with me, or this can get real ugly, real quick."

The laugh slithered through the street again, and the boy's body straightened. His shoulders pulled back, and his eyes widened, turning blue as a mountain lake. For a moment, Jesse James was gone, and the scrawny Jeb Fisher stood before him.

"Please, mister, save me. Don't let him take me—"

A swirling cloud of inky purple-black mist shrouded the boy, hiding him from sight. A moment later, it was gone, and Jesse James stood, eyes black, between his two men.

"You still want this to get ugly?" Came Jeb's wispy voice. "Just you against me and my boys?"

Frank's hand fell away from his pistol. He knew in his heart that this specter was even more powerful than the prospector, and his Holy-whiskey-filled bullets wouldn't even slow it down. The only bullet that would remained in his duster pocket, its green glow hidden from sight. He thought briefly about the lariat and cuffs, but knew he'd die before getting either close to Jeb.

And he realized at that moment how badly he wanted—needed—to take Jesse James' spirit without harming Jeb. He didn't have it in him to kill another child, to make another father mourn his son.

"Seems like you're undecided here, Mr. Butcher, so let me help you make up your mind."

He whistled and one of his men stepped out the hotel's front door with Camille hostage before him. She'd been gagged and bound, the rope slicing into the flesh of her wrists. Her eyes darted from Frank to Jeb and back again, no longer blank or empty.

"Now, looks to me like you and this…lady are quite fond of one another," Jesse hissed. He took Camille from his compatriot and pressed the muzzle of his gun to her head. "I'd hate to have to end a love affair between two corpses, but if you force my hand, I'll do it."

James moved back behind his gang on the steps to the hotel.

So, he was nervous, maybe even scared. Behind the gang, a shadow shifted in the hotel door.

"Seems like a Mexican standoff, then," Frank said. "I can't let you rob that bank, and you can't let me take you back to Hell."

James laughed again, keeping the gun to Camille's head. "You're too late to stop the robbery, Marshal. We just withdrew forty-thousand. None of it was ours, of course…"

"Then I can't let you get away."

"You're outgunned five to one, gun fighter," James said. "That's hardly a standoff. It's a slaughter."

Spike fired, bouncing a bullet off the dusty street at one crook's feet.

"Five to two," Frank growled.

James only shrugged. "Either way, she still dies, and likely both of you. Oh, and before things go too far here, you know that special bullet they gave you? The one with the right pretty green glow?"

Frank nodded, his hand twitching by his gun.

"Did you stop to wonder," James asked, "why there was only one in the box?"

For an instant, he pointed his pistol at Frank, just long enough for a greenish glow to show from each slot in the cylinder. Then he pressed it back against Camille's temple.

"So, we'll just take your saloon princess here and be on our way."

Frank tensed. "I can't let you do that, either. I'm taking you back to Hell one way or another, Jesse James."

He had to hope the Holy-whiskey-coated bullets would be enough. He was too far for the cuffs, and was no good with a lasso. He readied himself, forcing his body to relax, to smooth his draw. His heart ached at the thought of losing Camille, but she was already dead, after all. He'd see her in Hell.

Across from him, James cocked back the hammer on his gun. Camille looked Frank in the eye, fear and rage smoldering behind her gaze.

But his hand wouldn't move, wouldn't even touch the ivory handle of the six-shooter.

"What's the matter, Butcher?" James taunted, sounding very much like the child whose body he possessed. "Can't decide between duty and the whore?"

Frank lowered his hand. He couldn't take the shot. No matter what happened to Camille, Frank couldn't shoot another boy.

Movement stirred behind the gang again, and Curtis slipped out the door, reaching for the back pocket of his one-time friend. Frank looked away, but too late.

"Back off, you little shit!" James backhanded Curtis in the face, sending the smaller boy tumbling back inside the lobby.

That was all it took. The street exploded in gunfire.

The first shot came from Spike's Winchester as he took down a gang member reaching inside the lobby for Curtis. Frank drew and dove behind a watering trough, hitting the dirt just as bullets tore into the wood and zinged through the water inside. He peeked over the trough and took down a second bad guy, but had to get back under cover after that, as a storm of bullets tore through the air around him.

The gun fire drove Spike back until he hid behind the corner of the hotel. Frank managed to peer around the trough and check on his other two companions. Camille still stood in the grasp of James, though he'd dragged her to the right edge of the porch. Curtis remained out of sight, inside the hotel lobby.

A rider thundered around the corner near Spike, nearly knocking the barkeep off his feet, pulling five more horses and their wagon full of supplies behind him. James and his men jumped into the saddles, him pulling Camille up behind him, and turned to leave. Before galloping away, though, James looked back over his shoulder, grinning Jeb's slimy grin.

"Y'all know my friend, I believe," he taunted in his wispy, too-young voice. "He means to keep you from following me."

Frank jumped to his feet, taking aim at the boy's galloping horse, but then the doors exploded off the Dampier House, peppering Frank with shards and splinters. Standing where the doors had been, towering to the top of the door frame, the prospector glared out at them, his eyes obsidian in the noon sun. His face was contorted now, like a second, hideous face had pushed its way to the surface, demonic and mad with rage.

He held a shotgun in one hand, braced against his

hip, and his old revolver in the other.

Spike dove back behind the corner as the shotgun blasted away part of the siding. Frank rolled behind the trough again as forty-five caliber lead ripped and pinged around him.

The prospector laughed, the sound of a hundred demons rejoicing in death, reveling in the destruction of good. The shotgun roared again, and bullets ricocheted off the ground near Frank's head. The old man never seemed to run out of rounds, no matter how often he fired.

Then a voice, high and squeaky, hollered over the gunshots, making the prospector pause.

"Hey, old timer!" Curtis yelled from the exploded doorway. "You smell like a corpse!"

The delay gave Frank the moment he needed. Rising to one knee, he fired a Holy-whiskey-coated round, striking the prospector in the shoulder. The old man rocked, bellowing in agony as smoke rose from the wound. Frank fired again and again, hitting him in the chest and leg. Spike let loose from the corner, too, and in an instant, smoke rose from all over the old man's body, leaking from a half-dozen bullet holes.

He shrank, then, his body shriveling from its eight-foot height back to the crumpled, bent old man they'd seen in the pass outside Creede. His face remained grotesque, but he looked weak now. Decimated. His eyes opened wide with something Frank didn't expect: fear.

Dropping the shotgun, the old man took off running down Division Street, not looking back.

Frank rushed to the porch to find Curtis unharmed, panting but grinning from ear to ear.

"That was right stupid, boy," Frank scolded. "You could've been killed."

"But I wasn't." He held up a folded piece of paper for

Frank. "And I know where they're going next. We can get Camille back."

The paper—yellowed from smoke and age, like an old rancher's teeth—turned out to be a map of the Chicago, Rock Island, and Pacific Railroad, with a red circle drawn around Adair, Iowa.

Citizens had filed back into the street now, milling and whispering, and Frank could feel their eyes on him. Not needing any more attention, he folded the map and stuffed it in the pocket of his duster.

"All right, boys," Frank said, striding up the hotel steps. "Gather up your things and let's get some horses. We've got ground to cover."

CHAPTER ELEVEN

Horses turned out to be a bad idea. Frank had already paid for three and found out the hard way they dislike the smell of death, especially when it's climbing on their backs. They'd just started getting the horses calmed down when Batcho showed up and decided to scare them more, barking and yipping and growling until the mounts were uncontrollable. Then the coyote trotted off with what Frank swore was a smile on his face.

So they ended up getting their money back, minus a small fee for the inconvenience, and renting a private stage coach to Adair. They'd discussed taking the train, but never would have made it on time, having to stop in Des Moines. Short of changing horses halfway, the stage held their best hope of beating the new James gang to the spot.

Their only obstacle had been the wealthy family who'd already contracted the stage, but they got one whiff of Frank and Spike and decided to wait for the next day. Frank thought his cloud of black flies might have helped them decide, too.

Now the four of them—Frank, Spike, Curtis, and Batcho—sat on the worn leather seats of the stage as it thundered south. To their right, the setting sun drew long, distorted shadows across the prairie, golden grass swaying in the wind. The smells of old leather and dust filled the coach, but at least the horses couldn't smell the corpses they were hauling.

"Outside Adair's where the original gang tried their first train heist." Spike had talked to the stage driver before they left, learning everything he could from the man. "Killed two people—a conductor and the engineer. Only made about a third of what they thought, since the gold shipment they were after went on another train."

"So, another mistake being rectified," Frank muttered. "But there's more to this than just re-doing their fouled up robberies."

Spike nodded. "They stole forty-thousand dollars from the bank in Northfield. They have enough TNT to blow up a mountain. And they pick up men in every city. That's not for your average heist."

"Or no heist at all," Frank suggested. "Curtis, you got that newspaper I bought?"

The boy nodded and dug the rolled-up paper out from under his seat.

"Good," Frank told him. "Now look in the letters to the editor section and see what's there."

Curtis flipped through the paper, stopping a few pages in. His eyes went wide and his mouth formed an "O."

"How'd you know?" he asked.

Frank shrugged. "I didn't know much about Jesse when I was alive, but I recalled he was always writing letters to the papers. Go ahead, then...what's it say?"

Curtis scanned the page, shaking his head. "Seems like Mr. James thinks the south shoulda won the war. His letter kinda rambles about Union crimes against the south and how only his gang fights for the average southerner now, but he finishes with something strange: 'July 16th is our Independence Day, rooted in the clay from which we came and to which we will return forever. With the blood of our oppressors and that of innocents shall we rise again.'"

"So, this is all about the south getting what's theirs?" Spike asked, barely lifting his head from the leather cushion.

"Sure sounds like it," Frank answered. Batcho's ears perked up and he sniffed at the newspaper. "Jesse never did accept the south's defeat, so he probably blames the north for him going to Hell, too. If he robs from the north and gives to the south, he gets some revenge."

Batcho sniffed the paper again, this time growling and ruffling the fur on his neck. He looked at Frank, whined, then growled at the paper again.

"Damned coyote," Frank spat. "Other than biting the prospector, you've done us no good at all. You almost got us lost, scared those horses, and now you're growling at a newspaper. You're as worthless here as you were in the underworld."

Batcho sighed and put his chin on his paws.

An hour later, Curtis was snoring, his head on Spike's shoulder while the stout barkeep coated more bullets in what remained of their Holy-whiskey.

"You'd have made a fine father," Frank murmured.

Spike looked up and studied him through squinted eyes, his brow wrinkled so much the dead, dry skin cracked.

"That's why you couldn't shoot him, isn't it?" Spike asked. "Because he's in a kid's body and you…"

Frank looked out the window, into the growing darkness. The stage had slowed to avoid injuring the horses, but he could see little in the shadows.

"Leave it be," he warned.

"You can't dwell on that now. We need you."

Frank sighed and took his hat off long enough to run his fingers through his dead hair. It had started to soften a bit, as if life were slowly returning to his body one strand at a time.

"What would you know about it? You never shot your own boy."

"You didn't know," Spike reassured him. "You couldn't have—"

"Don't matter. I know what it's like to shoot a boy, and to lose one. Jeb Fisher is someone's boy, and if I can find a way, I'll capture James' spirit without killing the body it lives in. I owe his father that much, at least."

Curtis lifted his head and opened his bleary eyes. "His pa's dead. Died in the mines. Mom in childbirth. He's got no one to return to, and the boy I used to know…well, he ain't in there anymore. Kill him, Frank. You'll be helping him."

Spike clapped Frank on the shoulder.

"The judges sent a gunfighter on this mission, Frank. They had plenty of dead lawmen, plenty of bounty hunters, and plenty of other men. But they sent you. They knew your reputation and sent you because of it.

"You don't send a gunfighter to catch people, Frank. You send 'em to kill. If we're gonna win this, you'd better get to killin'."

CHAPTER TWELVE

They arrived at the train depot in Adair just before nine in the morning of their second day, their third set of horses lathered and huffing, their driver eying his passengers as if they were ghosts. Frank wondered if the man had any idea now close that was to the truth.

The station at Adair was a simple, steep-roofed building with white clapboard sides and no platform. Passengers milled around on the hard-packed dirt surface, their clothes caked in dust. Anvil clouds rose in the far west, though, threatening a soaking later. A single locomotive, gleaming and black, puffed smoke ahead of its mix of passenger and boxcars. Its whistle blew, making Curtis jump and Batcho tuck his tail.

"The robbery happened about a mile and a half west of town," Spike told the others. "There's a stone marker, commemorating those who died. I'll see if I can find a wagon to carry us the rest of the way."

"We'll walk," Frank said, starting down the road away from the depot. The train lurched forward at the same time, chugging west, its cars slow to move behind it, as if they longed to stay and rest at the depot.

Curtis took off at a run for the nearest boxcar. When he reached it, he ran along beside the train, matching its speed.

"This will be faster!" he shouted. "Come on, quick now!"

Spike grinned at Frank. "Grit."

Then he huffed and puffed his way alongside the boy. Frank sighed, then followed, Batcho yipping at his heels.

Spike grasped the handle on the boxcar door and heaved it open just as a shout rose from the depot. Spike hauled himself inside, then tugged Curtis in with him. The train had picked up speed now, and Frank struggled to keep up. He managed to grasp Spike's wrist, though, and the stronger man pulled him inside.

That left Batcho. The coyote ran alongside the train, moving as fast as his legs would move, scruffy tail streaming behind him like a banner.

"Jump!" Frank yelled. "We'll pull you in!"

But the coyote gave up, slowing to a trot, then a walk, then finally sitting beside the track, his tongue lolling out as he watched his companions go.

"Damned worthless coyote," Frank muttered.

"He'll find us," Spike said. "Inside that coyote head is the mind of an Indian guide."

Frank grunted, then sat with his legs dangling out the door. Curtis and Spike stood behind him in silence.

When the marker came into view on the side of the tracks, Frank heaved himself out of the car, rolling when he hit the grass-covered ground. Spike and Curtis followed, the boy doing surprisingly well, as if he'd jumped off trains before.

The three stood, waiting for the train to pass.

"What now?" Spike asked.

"Now, we wait." Frank snatched a long stalk of prairie grass and chewed on it, his hand resting on the handle of his pistol. "And when the James gang shows, we kill them, save Camille, and drag Jesse's spirit back to Hell, screaming."

Thunder clouds stalked in the distance, behind a small stand of trees, but the sky overhead was bluer than Frank had ever seen.

"We'd best hide in those trees," he said.

The shade cooled them, but did nothing to relieve the thick, wetness of the air.

Frank took up position behind an ancient oak, peering out around its fat, textured trunk to watch the tracks. Curtis and Spike sat, backs against trees, and closed their eyes.

"Last time they robbed a train here," Spike said, "they removed a section of track. Train crashed, people died. You reckon they'd make the same mistake again?"

Frank shrugged. "Don't know, but I don't suppose a soul condemned to Hell rightly cares who he kills in the living world."

"He cares," Curtis said, not even opening his eyes as he spoke. "He's trying to paint himself the hero, judging from that letter. Can't kill innocent people and still be a hero."

Spike raised an eyebrow at Frank. "Young man has a point."

Frank nodded. "You're proving more useful than that damned coyote guide. Just stay out of sight when the shooting starts. You're the only one of us with a life left to live."

"So, you three are really dead?" Curtis asked.

Frank nodded again, still watching the tracks in both directions. A smudge of smoke rose from the east.

"How'd you come back?"

Frank gave the boy the short version of their story, starting with the judges, and Curtis listened in silence, nodding his head from time to time. When Frank finished, the smoke on the horizon had grown and in the distance, a whistle blew. The train appeared as a thin, black worm sliding toward them across the rolling terrain.

"Frank?" Curtis didn't look at him, the boy's eyes far away and dark, like the undersides of the storm clouds coming in from the west.

Frank grunted.

"Since there's a Hell, you suppose there's a Heaven too?"

"Residents of Hell seemed to think so."

That painted a smile on the boy's lips, though his eyes remained far away. "Then that must be where my parents are. And it must mean I'll see 'em when I go there, too. They'll be waiting for me."

Staring at Curtis, Frank felt a bond with him, one he'd never had with his own boy. It made him question if bringing him along had been the right thing.

The train whistle blew again, and Frank readied himself.

"Well, you just stay hidden like I told you," he warned. "Don't be in such a hurry to make it out of this world."

Curtis didn't reply, but continued to stare off into the distance, like he could see his ma and pa waiting for him.

"We wait here until the James gang makes their move

on the train," Frank told Spike. "With any luck, we can catch them by surprise. Shoot for the head, especially if our prospector friend shows up. I'll handle Jesse myself."

He patted the lasso on his hip and the iron cuffs under his duster. He'd take the Fisher boy alive. Killing a child was not an option.

The locomotive was visible now, a gleaming black machine burping clouds of smoke, looking like it was bound for destination: Hell itself. The ground shook as it reached them, and the engineer blew the whistle again, making Curtis cover his ears. Frank studied the train and its surroundings, searching for any sign of the James gang. Flat cars, box cars, and hoppers clattered past on the track, with no sign of the gang or its leader. Finally, the caboose streaked by, a flash of red following a snake of browns and grays, and still the new James gang was nowhere to be seen.

As the caboose lumbered out of sight, Spike stood and stretched.

"That was a freight train anyway," he said, pacing around their little copse. "The gang preferred to rob passenger trains, so if the safe was empty, they could steal from the passengers."

Frank acknowledged him with a curt nod, but something in his gut felt wrong. He went over things in his mind, from the map to what the gang had done so far. Adair had been circled on the map. Like Creede and Northfield, it marked a wrong Jesse needed to make right. It was almost too perfect, and for an instant, Frank wondered if it was a trap.

He shook off the feeling. This had to be it.

So, like Spike, he paced their hideaway, only Curtis still lounging against a tree. The day wore on, the sun turning their shaded spot into an oven, and the clouds rolled closer, pushing the humidity up until Frank thought he could have taken bites of the air. Mosquitoes found them, whining in his ear and trying to bite him, mingling with the constant swarm of flies. Curtis swatted and swiped to keep them off him, but Frank and Spike didn't have to bother. Bites would heal before starting to itch.

The next train blew its whistle around three hours after the first, startling Curtis from a light sleep and making Frank look west, where a tendril of smoke rose to merge with the gray of the cloud base above it. Flashes of lightning lit up the clouds, and the train sped east, fleeing the wrath of the storm.

This was a short, sleek passenger train that streaked by them in just a few seconds, not even slowing, its passengers staring out their windows, unaware Frank and his comrades were staring back.

As the passenger train slipped east into the wavy hills around Des Moines, Frank cussed under his breath.

"Still no sign of the gang," he muttered. "I'm starting to think we got the wool pulled over our eyes."

"There's one more westbound passenger train due in ninety minutes," Curtis said. "The Des Moines to Omaha evening run. I asked around at the depot, and it normally carries armed Army officers, so I'm betting it has a gold shipment."

"You couldn't have mentioned this earlier?" Spike asked.

"Sorry," Curtis said. "Frank had his mind set on waiting here."

Frank rolled his eyes, but sure enough, ninety minutes later, as the sun dipped behind the storm clouds and a few drops of rain pattered the grove around them, a train whistle blew to their east. Lightning flashed and a few seconds later, thunder pealed across the plains. Frank's gut twisted — the thunder seemed somehow prophetic, like some sort of omen or warning that evil rode on the clouds and that the world of the living should move aside and make way.

The train came into sight over a hill, smoke erupting from its stack as it sped across the open plain. With the sun almost down and the lightning their only true source of illumination, Frank caught only glimpses of the locomotive, with its light a shining eye in the dark between flashes. Slowly, the train's roar took hold in Frank's knees.

"They should be here," Spike said, looking both directions along the track. "If they're going to rob this train, they should be in position by now."

"Something doesn't feel right," Frank replied. "We should — "

"What's that?" Curtis jumped to his feet and pointed at the oncoming train. "There, on top of the cars!"

Frank squinted into the growing darkness, and at first he saw nothing. Then lightning flashed, splitting a tree just across the tracks from them, and Frank saw what the boy was talking about. There, standing tall atop the first passenger car, tattered flannel flapping in the wind, stood the prospector. Even at a hundred yards, the old man looked eight feet tall, maybe more, and his eyes seemed to absorb the darkness around him, getting blacker than they'd ever been. His ghost-white hair streamed out behind him. He held his pickaxe to the sky, challenging the lightning to take its best shot at striking him down.

Frank's first instinct was to hide, but the prospector stared right at him, and he knew without a doubt he'd been spotted. He drew his six-shooter, ejected one round, and inserted the green-glowing bullet, his weapon of last resort. He flipped the cylinder closed and spun it until the special round would be the last he fired. He preferred not to waste it on anyone but Jesse James, but something told him it might be all that stopped the old man this time.

He handed the cuffs to Spike.

"I'll handle this," he growled as the wind picked up and the rain started to pummel the earth around them. "You two stay safe. Get away if you can."

"Hell no," Spike said.

"Someone's gotta rescue Camille," Frank argued. "In case I don't make it out of this gunfight on my own."

The train was almost on them now, and Frank stepped out of the trees to take on the prospector from Hell. The wind stole his hat, but Frank let it go.

To his surprise, the prospector leapt from the passenger car, landing in a crouch a few feet away, tossing aside the bloody pick. When he started to rise, Frank drew and aimed at his head. The prospector froze, and an icy laugh hacked its way from his lungs.

"You still think you can kill me with a fancy bullet, gunfighter? That's why I used a living body. Unlike your corpse, it can change. Evolve."

Frank cocked the hammer on his Colt in answer.

The prospector laughed again, the sound of ice cracking on a frozen lake.

"Even your friend with the Winchester over in those trees knows that won't work."

"Where's Jesse James?" Frank barked. "I'm here to return him to Hell where he belongs."

The prospector rose up to his full height, towering over Frank by two or three feet.

"Jesse and the boys went on ahead. They told me to come and be your welcoming party."

His gut had been right—it was a trap.

"Then get to welcomin'," Frank said, "so I can move on and do my job."

The prospector drew his revolver so fast Frank barely had time to fire. The bullet tore into the old man's left shoulder, rocking him back. Unlike the last whiskey-coated round, though, this one had no other effect. No smoke, no shrinking. Nothing.

Frank dove right as the prospector fired off a three-round burst that sent up wads of dirt and grass. Frank rose to his knee and fired two more shots, both striking the prospector in the chest. Again, though, the old man simply rocked back, then fired again. No shrinking. No pain.

Frank rolled and saw Spike and Curtis running for the speeding train. The prospector turned to aim at them, and Frank fired his last coated bullet at his back.

This time, the Holy-whiskey worked, making the prospector arch his back and fall to one knee. Seeing his chance, Frank holstered his gun and ran. He lowered his shoulder, ready to drive it into the wound in the old man's back, but the prospector was ready for him. At the last instant, he wheeled, grabbed Frank by his duster, and flung him at the speeding train. Frank fell just short of the tracks, balling up to keep his limbs from being run over as the last car thundered past.

The prospector fell on him like a rabid dog, snarling and foaming, his black eyes full of hatred and bloodlust. The fingers of one huge hand closed around Frank's throat, while the other held his right hand—his gun hand—down against the ballast of the track.

The two wrestled for control, but the prospector had the edge. As Frank watched Curtis and Spike jump onto the caboose, he felt his world going black. He tried to reach for his gun with his left hand, but the prospector held him still.

"Foolish judges sent the wrong man," the prospector growled. Spit dripped from his mouth onto Frank's forehead, where it burned, despite the rain on his brow. "After I destroy you, I'll welcome your friends, too. I'll enjoy hurting the boy."

Fire erupted in Frank's heart, and with the last ounce of strength in his left hand, he grabbed the lasso off his hip and looped it around the prospector's neck. The old man's midnight eyes went wide and he clawed at the rope. That freed Frank's hands. In a single motion, he drew his Colt, put it under the old man's chin, and fired the green bullet.

The prospector's head snapped back, his body flying from Frank in a flash of misty, green light. He landed with a thud a few yards away, writhing on the ground as glowing, serpentine mist flowed around his arms and legs. On its own, the lasso tightened around his neck.

The light disappeared and the world fell silent. Even the thunder seemed muffled and distant. Frank rose to his knees, afraid to do anything but stare.

To his dismay, the prospector sat up, an evil grin spreading across his face like oil across a pond. His fingers grasped the lasso and started to loosen it.

"Fool," he snarled.

Lightning flashed and the sound of the train returned, shaking the ground. Frank looked for the train, wondering how Spike had talked them into backing up, but a second burst of lightning showed him the true source of the noise.

A massive tornado wove its way toward him from the west, green light flashing and swirling inside it as the funnel danced its way across the plain. Frank ran, throwing himself in a ditch a few yards away just as a tree flew past him like a giant skewer. He wrapped his arms around a stout stump and held on for dear life.

The twister came to a stop over the prospector, and for a moment, the green lightning within it seemed to do battle with that around his body. The old man jumped to his feet and tried to run, but a bolt of green lightning shot down from the clouds, hammering through him. He stood, arms out, eyes wide, and screamed as the lightning burned through his body.

Then, he just disappeared.

An instant later, the funnel withdrew into the clouds and the storm moved off to the east.

Still in the ditch, Frank put his head down and let darkness swallow him.

CHAPTER THIRTEEN

Frank woke to the buzz of flies and the smothering heat of the sun on his back. The earthy smell of loam nudged his senses and he tasted the grit of dirt in his mouth.

Cracking his eyes open one at a time, he found himself face-down in the ditch, his hair matted to his head, hat long gone. He pushed himself to a sitting position, surprised to find himself alone and still in one piece. Rain had soaked through his duster, so he took it off to dry.

He crawled to the lip of the ditch. Clear, blue skies dominated from horizon to horizon, though the smoke tendril of a train rose to the east, a lone scar on nature's otherwise flawless face. The stand of trees in which they'd hidden the night before looked like a tangle of green and brown, now, trunks tied in knots by the tornado.

The twister. The prospector. Frank couldn't wrap his mind around what he'd seen, what he'd caused. He'd wiped a soul from existence, killing not only its possessed body, but eradicating the essence itself.

Needing his mind off the subject, he checked his Colt, reloading with regular bullets. One remaining whiskey-coated bullet in his gun belt was now his only ammunition against Jesse James, should he manage to come across him. Spike still had the cuffs, and the lasso had disappeared into the clouds with the prospector's body.

He'd have to choose the when and where for using the bullet—he'd only get one shot.

Levering himself to his feet, he re-holstered his piece, threw his duster over his shoulder, and started west. He had to find Spike and Curtis. A flutter of movement caught his eye, just to the north. But someone—or something, he thought, down on all fours—slipped into a grove of trees and disappeared, little more than a shadow receding into more shadows.

"Looks like I have company," he mumbled to himself.

He trudged west along the tracks all morning, catching the occasional glimpse of his pursuer, always just inside his peripheral vision for an instant before slipping through the tall grass like a phantom. He seemed to want Frank to know he was there, watching him. Either that or he was taunting him, flaunting the fact that he tracked his prey and there was nothing Frank could do about it.

Frank stopped briefly at noon, resting under the shade of a willow, letting his body rebuild a bit, then headed west again.

Dusk had made its dusty, gray entrance when a stagecoach appeared on the western horizon, a black speck kicking up dust against the glowing orange disk of the sun.

Frank looked for somewhere to get out of sight until the coach passed, but the nearest trees stood fifty yards away, and the coach was approaching fast.

So he put on his duster, angled away from the coach, and plodded forward.

But the stage turned toward him, so Frank stopped and faced it head-on.

About thirty yards away, the driver whistled and reined in his four-horse team, skidding to a stop right in front of Frank. He was a young man, with a hungry look in his blue eyes and a rifle across his lap. Frank let his hand rest on his pistol.

"He's here," the driver said, his voice taut like a new-strung fence wire. "He's alive, but he doesn't look too happy."

The stage door opened and Frank tensed, ready to draw at the slightest sign of trouble. He relaxed when Spike jumped down from the step, Curtis on his heels. The boy took one look at Frank and dashed to him, wrapping his arms around Frank's waist.

Feeling awkward, Frank tousled Curtis' hair and eased him back. Tears glistened in Curtis's eyes, and he wiped at them furiously, turning away.

"I thought the prospector…"

"You oughta have more faith in me, boy," Frank scolded playfully. "Takes more than one old man to kill Frank Butcher."

Spike gave him a questioning look.

Frank shook his head. "The prospector won't be hassling us anymore. But I had to use that one bullet I wasn't supposed to use."

Spike raised his eyebrows, then shrugged and handed the cuffs back to Frank.

"Well, you owe me a nickel, Curtis," the barrel-chested barkeep said. "I told you Frank would win."

The boy handed over a coin, making a show of disgruntlement, but unable to hide his ear-to-ear grin at finding Frank alive.

"Mister, you know you're being followed?" The driver hefted his rifle — a Sharps carbine — as if to take aim. Frank held him up with wave of his hand.

"Been following me all day and hasn't made a move yet. Let's just put some distance between us and him."

"You get a good look at him?" the driver asked. Frank shook his head. "Me either, but get in and we'll leave him so far behind he can't remember who you are."

Frank and the others climbed inside, the driver cracked the whip, and the stage started rolling. They did a three-quarters turn and headed south. Frank gave Spike a wondering look, but Curtis explained.

"We found out where the gang is going. Looks like Liberty, Missouri is the site of their next heist. And they picked up some new members, too. There are about twenty of 'em now. Maybe more."

"And Camille?"

"Still with 'em," Spike said.

Around midnight, Frank realized the stage had neither slowed nor stopped since he'd boarded, maintaining a steady southward trot down the narrow dirt road. Spike and Curtis were sleeping, so Frank leaned his head out the window and called out to the driver.

"How long until you change horses at this pace?"

The driver turned to face Frank, his eyes glowing a fierce, ice-cold blue, the stark red ash from a cigarette dangling from his lips.

"These ones don't need changed." The voice was the same one he'd heard earlier, just made colder by the glowing blue eyes. "Come on up and I'll show you."

Frank opened the door and swung himself around and up into the seat to the driver's left. Up close, his eyes held more detail: varying shades of blue, a dark pupil, even flecks of silver. But they still glowed.

The driver held out his hand.

"Stanley Dobbs," he said. Frank shook his hand, surprised to find it warm and alive. "Stan. Oh, I'm alive, all right. I just have access to certain…powers that most people don't. The eyes allow me to see in the dark, like a cat, only better."

"Frank Butcher, Stanley. You wanna tell me what you mean about these horses?"

"Did you notice that they weren't spooked by you walking corpses, like normal horses are?"

Frank nodded, even though it had slipped his attention.

"That's because these beauties aren't your everyday horses, Frank. Look close."

Frank leaned down, near the rear flank of the closest horse. He could feel the horse's body heat, but there was something else, something unusual.

The horse looked back over its shoulder and Frank nearly fell from the seat. The animal's eyes held the faintest, tiniest sparks of orange in them, as if embers floating from a fire had lodged themselves there. If he hadn't been looking, he likely wouldn't have noticed, But he'd seen those types of eyes in a horse before: in the underworld.

"You mean they…"

"Yep, you got it, Frank. These thoroughbreds come straight from the underworld, the realm of the dead. They can run for hours, if needed, then run some more. They should have us in Liberty by tomorrow night."

Frank sat back on the bench, looked at the driver's glowing eyes, and sighed.

"Who sent you?"

Stan laughed, a quick, honest sound that put Frank at ease.

"The judges, of course. They learned of the prospector's presence here and figured you could use some help getting around."

"They've been spying on me?"

"Did you expect anything less?"

Frank kicked himself for not expecting some sort of over-watch by the judges, especially Webber. They weren't exactly the trusting types.

"So, they knew things were going south in and sent you to help?"

"Yep, it's good old Stan Dobbs to the rescue."

"How do they arrange for someone in the world of the living to help to with matters of the dead?"

"Everything has its price, gunfighter. You just gotta know the currency." He sat up straight and stuffed his hand in his vest pocket. "Which reminds me, I paid a pretty penny for this. Hope you appreciate it."

He handed Frank a piece of paper and a match. Frank struck the match and shielded it with his hand, using its light to read the Western Union telegram:

Whoever you are, not interested in life of crime. Retired now. Leave me alone.

- FJ

The match burned out and he was in darkness again.

"That was sent from Saint Louis to Omaha for a Mr. Thomas Howard."

Frank shrugged. The name meant nothing to him.

"That's one of the aliases Jesse used when he was alive. FJ is his brother Frank, telling him he won't be joining him in his little group."

"Finally, something went our way," Frank said. "Now if we can just pick up a dozen more members of this little posse…"

"Well, you got me. I ain't much, but I shoot straight, even in the dark." Stan looked him over from head to toe, sniffed, and made a clucking sound. "You'd better get back down there and rest. Your reanimated bodies need — whoa!"

He reined in hard, the horse team whinnying and rearing up as they skidded to a stop in the middle of the trail. Frank's gun came out, and the driver lifted his Sharps rifle to his shoulder.

"What is it?" Frank asked.

"Something crossed the road in front of us," Stan whispered. "About twenty yards ahead. I think it was your shadow, down on all fours. Huge, like the size of a bull."

"What is it?"

The driver put his fingers to his temples and closed his eyes, leaving just slivers of blue. He concentrated for a moment, then opened his eyes again.

"Can't be certain. But I think you got a Hellhound chasing you."

The doors opened, and Frank snapped to Spike and Curtis. "Stay inside! We got company you don't wanna meet."

"It doesn't make sense," Stan said. "Jesse James shouldn't have been able to bring a Hellhound into the world of the living. He doesn't have that kind of power. Only…"

He let the though trail off, like a path to nowhere. Frank cleared his throat.

"How do we deal with it now?"

"It's gone now," Stan said. "I don't see it at all, but it left something in the road in front of us."

Frank dismounted, six-gun held before him. He looked back at Stan and Spike, both of whom had their rifles trained into the darkness ahead of him.

Frank still didn't know what to think of Stan, whether or not he could trust him, so Spike's support was comforting. He took a step.

"Straight ahead, about fifteen yards now." Stan kept his voice low.

The prairie around them sat cool and still, the waving of the grass all that disturbed the night's graveyard calm. The moon hadn't risen yet, either, leaving Frank blind.

"Few more yards," Stan said. "You should see it soon."

And he did. There, sitting in the right hand wheel rut, was Frank's hat, its black satin band caked with mud. The raven's feather had gone missing, but the hat looked otherwise the same.

Cautiously, searching the tall grass for any sign of movement, Frank bent and picked up his hat. He inspected the inside, found it acceptably clean, and stuffed it back on his head. Then he trudged to the stage and climbed up next to Stan again. The driver snapped the reins and the wagon lurched forward.

"A Hellhound delivered your hat?" Stan arched his eyebrows over the crystalline blue of his eyes. "I think I'd have left it there."

As they trotted through the inky black of night, Frank shrugged.

"I like my hat."

CHAPTER FOURTEEN

By the time they trotted into Liberty the next day, the sun was setting in a sea of fire to their west as another round of storms built over the plains, preparing for their assault eastward. Brilliant purples and oranges, reds and umbers painted the horizon, while darkness grew in the cobbled streets of Liberty, with its two-and-three-story buildings.

Frank couldn't enjoy the colors, though, for his body felt ready to collapse, as if every ounce of life had seeped into the ground or evaporated into the air. He'd kept watch the whole trip, trying to spot the Hellhound, and it had taken its toll on him. He could feel his body deteriorating. The coach wheeled to a stop outside a hotel, Stan hopping down to open the door for Spike and Curtis. Frank dragged himself from the bench, nearly collapsing when his feet hit the ground.

Spike didn't look much better as he forced his huge frame out of the coach.

Stan tossed Frank a skeleton key.

"Room 3C. Got get some rest. Your bodies need some down time. Curtis and I will get something to eat." He led Curtis by the elbow away from the hotel. "Not all of us can go without food, you know?"

Frank still didn't trust the driver, but was too tired to argue, so he climbed the steps.

"And we need to see a man about a horse," Curtis blabbed. "Some information from a reliable source or two."

Stan tried to shush him, but Frank had already stopped in his tracks.

"No! It's too dangerous. Once we're rested —"

"By the time you're rested," Curtis argued, "it'll be too late. Besides, no one will talk to a gunfighter, especially a smelly one matching your description, but they'll spill just about anything to a boy. After all, what harm could that do?"

He flashed a grin of exaggerated innocence. Frank wanted to argue, but lacked the energy. Besides, the boy was probably right—he had a better chance at finding information than Frank did, and time was running short.

"All right, go ahead. But you listen to Stan here. There are enough corpses in this posse already." He fired a warning glare at the driver. "Anything happens to him, and you'll get to meet those judges in person sooner than you'd expect."

Stan paled and swallowed hard.

"He's in good hands."

And off they went into the growing darkness.

Frank and Spike trudged up the stairs to their third-floor room, locked the door behind them, and collapsed.

Frank fell into a cushioned chair, propping his feet up on a chaise, while Spike flopped onto the lone bed and was snoring within minutes. Frank took in the room's smoke-stained wallpaper, single window, and had just started nodding off when a dog barked.

Batcho? He pushed himself out of the chair and moved to the window. It opened over a dark, dank alley behind the hotel, a place Frank would not want to walk, even as someone already dead. A black-and-white mutt whined and slinked off down the alley, into the dark.

The hair on the back of Frank's neck rose. Goosebumps prickled his skin as a shadow detached itself from a corner of the alley, stepping into the dim light cast by his open window. The Hellhound glared up at him with eyes of yellow fire, and let out a low, hate-filled growl. Frank gasped at the sheer enormity of the beast, easily four feet at the shoulders, and as big around as Spike.

Frank squinted and thought he could make out finger-length fangs under the fierce, hateful glow of its eyes. Then the hound turned and bound away down the alley, disappearing into the shadows.

Frank shivered and closed the window, locking it tight, as if that would stop something that huge. Then, he collapsed in his chair again.

This time, he slept.

* * *

He awoke to the sound of someone wiggling a key in the lock on their door, or picking the lock—he wasn't sure which. So he rolled out of the chair, drew his pistol, and cocked back the hammer just as the door inched open and a golden blade of light sliced into the room.

Whispered voices tiptoed over the rough sound of

Spike's rhythmic breathing.

The door edged open, bit by bit, until it revealed two figures standing outside. Frank stood and took aim at the larger one's head.

"Frank?" Curtis asked. "It's just us. Me 'n Stan."

Frank exhaled in a rush and lowered his pistol. The boy's voice woke Spike, who turned up the oil lamp beside the bed.

Sighing, Frank dropped into the chair again. Stan stepped in and closed the door behind him.

"I don't recall being this paranoid when I was alive," Frank said, wishing for a drink.

He told them all about the Hellhound, causing Stan to dash to the window and peer out into the night with his glowing blue eyes. Then he waved his hands around the frame and muttered under his breath. When done, he turned to Frank.

"It's gone." His brow furrowed and he looked like his mind was somewhere else. "But it'll be back. It should have trouble seeing through the window now."

Frank nodded. "What did you find out?"

Curtis and Stan swapped a look that said neither of them wanted to go first. Frank was about to ask when a knock sounded on the door.

Frank started to draw again, but the boy held up his hands in a calming gesture.

"It's all right. We're expecting him. He wants to help."

He moved toward the door.

"Just who the Hell is this—"

Curtis swung the door open and standing in the hall, haloed by the brighter light, was the bowler-wearing detective they'd met on the train, his moustache just as thick as it had been that day. His eyes appraised the room in a single sweep, and when he stepped inside, his brass badge shone.

"Charlie Mills, Detective."

"The Pinkerton man?" Frank raised his eyebrows. "Just what we need."

"Yeah," Spike chimed in, hostility lacing his voice like ivy around a trellis. "Don't you have mine workers to rough up or something? What do you want with our little party?"

Mills closed the door behind him.

"I was sent to investigate rumors of a possible gang of rebel sympathizers here in the Kansas River area. I overheard this youngster asking questions about one of my suspects, Jeb Fisher.

"So, young Curtis and I had a conversation that led us both to believe we share a common interest in seeing Mr. Fisher — or whoever he is — stopped."

Frank exchanged a look with Spike, the bartender raising an eyebrow.

"What do you mean, 'whoever he is?'"

Mills studied Frank with a trained eye that shone with years of experience judging people.

"Your two young friends here either have a knack for tall tales or have seen some pretty strange things." The detective sniffed the air, his moustache twitching. "And judging by the aroma coming off you two, and what I saw your coach driver do outside, I'm not inclined to dismiss them off-hand, though I admit some skepticism."

Frank shot the two a reproachful glare, but Curtis still grinned, his teeth shining like lanterns.

"You said we needed help, so I brought help. You could at least show a little thanks...what better help than a Pinkerton man?"

Having the agency's assets at their disposal would be helpful in dealing with the new James gang. If they could trust him, and that was a big "if."

"My agency was in pursuit of the James boys at one point. We have experience dealing with his type, so if Mr. Fisher is a copycat, we could be of assistance in stopping him."

"Pursuit?" Spike said, rolling his eyes. "Didn't your boys kill Jesse's half-brother and blow his mother's arm off?"

Mills winced like he'd been slapped, but recovered in a flash.

"No one positively tied our men to that…horrible accident," he said, choosing his words like snakes from a basket. "We deny all—"

Frank cut him off. "Yeah, yeah, we don't have time for your excuses. What you heard from Curtis there is true, Jesse James' soul escaped from Hell and it's our job to lasso him back down there. What can you do to help us?"

Mills raised an eyebrow.

Frank grunted and rolled up his sleeve, showing him where his skin had started to rot again. When that failed to impress the detective, Frank peeled off a fingernail and watched as it grew back immediately.

"Why don't we just assume you're telling the truth?" Mills said. "That way we can skip over my detective's need for hard evidence and get right to preventing this uprising."

Frank nodded. "And we'll just assume you're trustworthy, too."

"All right," Mills went on, "tell me what you've learned about Mr. Fisher's plans."

Frank told him everything he could remember, from the killing of Bob Ford and the load of dynamite to the robbery in Northfield and the growing gang. He also mentioned Camille, the prospector, and the statements about taking back what's rightfully theirs, Liberty, and the Clay from which they'd come. He chose to omit the part about the Hellhound. When he finished, Mills leaned back against the door, stuffed a wad of chew in his mouth, and ruminated at the ceiling.

After a few minutes, he stood and paced to the window, where he gazed out into the night. Frank hoped the Hellhound would make an appearance, just to frighten the detective into believing their story.

"It all adds up," he said, not looking away from the window. Frank disliked his flair for the dramatic. "Clay County is where Jesse's family came from, but the Union eventually ran them out of there, and Liberty refers to this town, the seat of Clay County.

"We received information a week ago that subversive elements from Clay County were going to try to rob union-associated banks, possibly in retaliation for the north's treatment of the James family or as revenge for the death of little Archie and the maiming of Zerelda James.

"First National hired my agency, and based on the Northfield robbery, we picked up Jeb Fisher's name and followed it here. But so far, no robberies, despite all that dynamite."

Frank stood and paced the room like the detective, scratching the spot on his chin where stubble would normally grow if he were alive.

"Wasn't Jesse part of a rebel militia group during the war?"

Mills nodded. "Quantrill's Raiders. And he followed Bloody Bill Anderson after that. Those two groups wreaked quite a bit of havoc along the Kansas-Missouri border."

"Bill Anderson was brutal," Spike said. "He used to wear a necklace of union scalps around his neck."

It all made sense to Frank now. The dynamite, the gang, the money. And the presence in Clay County. Even the letter in the paper fit.

"He's not just trying to bring down the local government," he muttered, loud enough for all to hear. "He's trying to re-start the war, gain revenge, and bring the south back to power."

Mills gave him another skeptical look. "Think about it," Frank explained. "Whether you believe James is back or that this is a copycat, it all adds up. He sets off some bombs, kills some government leaders, and terrorizes some pro-union citizens. Once he's convinced people the government can't protect them and avenged old perceived wrongs, the tinder for change is dry and ready to ignite.

"Then the Army moves in, and they make matters worse by making all these pro-rebel citizens feel oppressed, and suddenly the ranks of his militia grow."

The other three stared at him, mouths open.

"I served, too," he explained. "Union Army down in Texas. Both sides did this kind of thing."

"All right, how do we stop them?" Mills asked.

Frank shrugged. "That ain't our job. We're here to take one soul back to Hell, nothing more."

"So, I'm on my own?"

"I didn't say that," Frank said. "Seems to me we have a lot in common, even if our end goals ain't exactly the same. How many men can you get to fight the gang?"

Mills counted on his fingers. "Including me...one."

Frank shot him a flat stare, but chuckled inwardly. The man had pluck to get flip with a gunfighter from Hell. "What do you bring to the table, then, partner? Besides that girly British pistol tucked in the back of your pants."

Mills blushed a bit, his hand straying part way to the

gun. Then he regained his composure.

"I know their target."

CHAPTER FIFTEEN

Frank leaned against the corner of Goldman's Grocer on the south side of Town Square, looking north at the red brick of the Clay County courthouse building. With its white clock tower and dark dome, it sat alone on a plot of grass and trees, as if someone had dropped the entire symmetrical space down in the middle of the city. Atop the dome, a white marble statue of lady justice stood watch, wraith-like against the cold pallor of the Missouri sky.

"They say it's the finest courthouse in the state." Mills stood a few feet away, a smoke hanging under his bushy moustache. Above them, in the window of the Thompson House Hotel, Spike cleared his throat. Frank had set the barkeep and Stan there, ready to use the Winchester and Sharps to take out any gang members Frank and Mills couldn't handle.

Only, no gang members had shown up yet. The front of the courthouse buzzed with people, but so far, nothing unusual had taken place, and noon had passed an hour ago, when the clouds had rolled in and the temperature dropped like lead in a pond.

"You sure about this?" Frank asked. He'd started doubting the detective's motives.

Mills nodded. "Our source was very specific. Former Governor Crittenden is supposed to meet with an associate here this afternoon to discuss a business arrangement."

Frank squinted into the gray afternoon, trying to see what was happening on the covered balcony between the two protruding wings of the courthouse. Shadows made it difficult, but he saw nothing out of the ordinary. Not what he'd expect if a secret meeting with a former governor was going on. Especially a former governor who'd put a bounty on the heads of the original James gang. A bounty that got Jesse killed.

Citizens still entered and exited the building, too, conducting the routine business of any courthouse: marriages, taxes, and so on.

It didn't add up. Things were *too* routine.

The sun was setting behind a wall of slate-gray clouds that leaked drizzle on Liberty when the former governor's black lacquered coach finally arrived. The carriage glittered with raindrops as it pulled up to the south side of the courthouse, its two-horse team pawing at the ground and huffing.

Frank watched as the governor stepped out of the coach, his white hair waving in the breeze. In the distance, lightning flashed behind the courthouse, making it look like a giant grave marker or mausoleum.

Crittenden used both hands on the coach's rails, the ground apparently slick with rain. He strode up the short courthouse steps and through the front door without fanfare. No one even came to meet him.

There was still no sign of the James gang, either.

A few minutes later, Curtis came running down Kansas Street, sliding to a stop on the slippery street just a foot from Frank.

"Something's going on at the college," he huffed, hands on knees.

"At Jewell?" Mills asked.

Curtis shook his head. "Not Jewell. The Ladies' College. Really weird things."

Frank exchanged a look with Mills, whose brow had furrowed under his bowler. He seemed genuinely surprised.

"Tell us what you saw," Frank said.

"The Ladies College is at the west end of Franklin," the boy told them, "and from what I gather, normally it's pretty quiet right about now. They have an early curfew there, seeing that they're ladies and all.

"But tonight there are women-folk out all over the yard and on the balconies. And at least some of them have guns."

"I reckon we oughtta check it out," Frank told Mills.

"Agreed."

"Okay, Curtis," Frank said. "Lead the way."

They called down Spike and Stan from the hotel and climbed onto Stan's stage in Town Square, Frank and Mills on the driver's bench with Stan. They trotted north, past the courthouse on Main Street, and were just about to turn west on Franklin when a carriage thundered past, its four-horse team not even slowing for the other coach. Guards rode front and back, rifles held ready.

"I know that carriage," Mills said. "That's Mr. Pinkerton's private coach. He takes it anytime he wants to travel discretely."

The carriage rushed west down Franklin, straight toward the ladies college.

"Didn't Crittenden hire your agency to go after the James-Younger gang?" Frank asked.

Mills' eyes went wide and his mouth fell open. "He's gonna kill Mr. Pinkerton."

Something still didn't add up for Frank, though.

"Are you sure that was Crittenden at the courthouse?" he asked Mills.

The detective thought a moment, then looked at Frank, eyes narrowed.

"He didn't have a briefcase. Crittenden's an attorney. He wouldn't go to a business meeting without a briefcase."

"We've been hustled," Frank said. "Catch that coach!"

Stan whipped his team into a gallop, their red eyes blazing through the darkness as the group gave chase.

CHAPTER SIXTEEN

Frank held the side rail for dear life as Stan drove his horses hard enough for gouts of flame to erupt from their nostrils. They had to stop Pinkerton before he reached the college and went inside. Then, James would have everything he needed to start his rebellion and launch the second civil war.

But Pinkerton's coach had too much of a head start, and a few moments later, it pulled up the hill in front of the college. Stan reined in just short of the gate, a good hundred yards away, at the bottom of the hill.

Curtis had been right about the people milling around outside the school, despite the late hour. All were dressed like women—dark, ankle-length skirts, white blouses—but many carried themselves more like men. And held rifles. All stared blankly ahead.

Spike leaned out a window, and the four of them watched Pinkerton disembark and stride up the steps to the front door, disappearing inside.

"What do we do now?" Spike asked.

Frank studied the long hill up to the brick building that made up the college, taking in the large number of women — or people dressed like women, anyway — standing guard, despite the now-pouring rain. Frank directed Stan to take cover in a small stand of trees, where they got out and peered at the front of the ladies college.

A group of armed men hurried the Pinkerton carriage around behind the college, knocking the guards unconscious and dragging them into the building.

Frank put his hand on Mills' arm. The man was wound tight as a bear trap, ready to spring, but Frank held him back.

"Not yet," he whispered.

Mills frowned, but nodded. Frank's trust in him grew as he felt the man's anger boiling under the surface.

A light came on in the south end of the building, and Mills handed Frank a telescope. Through it, Frank watched Crittenden and Pinkerton take their seats at a table before a woman with blond hair closed the drapes. She paused for a moment, staring out into the night rain with dazzling blue eyes.

Frank tensed. "Camille."

Then she disappeared, leaving only a sliver of light visible.

Several of the women — including one who Frank swore had a full beard and moustache — moved to that corner of the building and crouched, working on something Frank couldn't make out.

"What're they doing?" he muttered.

Mills tapped him on the shoulder and pointed to a

low shed on the north side of the building. Frank used the telescope again. There, huddled against the rain, sat the now-empty wagon the James gang had used to haul their dynamite.

Motion at the opposite corner of the building caught Frank's eye as three more women knelt there, working feverishly on the base of the wall. Even with the looking scope, Frank couldn't see what they were doing. He didn't need to.

"They're blowing the whole thing," he said. "They're gonna kill the governor, Pinkerton, and a bunch of women. If that don't start the war, nothing will."

Mills straightened, reached into the coach and produced Camille's Winchester. He chambered a round and nodded. Spike held his shotgun against his hip, expression grim as he faced the college. Stan hefted the Sharps, his eyes blazing blue.

Only Curtis looked unsure, his gaze jumping from the school to Frank and back again.

"Stay here." Frank handed the boy the telescope. "Keep an eye on things, and if you see anyone—especially your friend Jeb—escaping, follow them. Stay safe, and don't let them see you, but find out where they go and report back to me at the hotel.

"Stan, you're with Curtis here, but use that rifle and those eyes of yours to give us cover fire. Curtis here can tell you if someone's…not normal. If anyone gets close to your position, skedaddle. Save yourselves. And if something happens to me…"

"I'll take care of Curtis."

Frank gave him a curt nod, then Stan and Curtis climbed atop the stage, the boy looking through the telescope. A moment later, he turned to Frank.

"Save her, okay?" he said. "She really needs to stay

here."

"I'll try." Frank turned to Mills and Spike. "Let's go."

He stepped out into the full force of the pouring rain. Dim oil lamps around the yard and porches lit the area enough to make out shapes of the guards walking about.

They marched up the hill, unabashed and unhidden, daring someone to open up on them. A quick count told Frank at least forty remained outside, drenched in the pouring rain.

"There are too many of them to be just the gang," Mills said. "Something doesn't add up."

Frank grunted. "Spread out. I'll get James, you two stop the dynamite."

As they split, the front door burst open, spilling golden light out across the hillside, turning the women into silhouettes. Then James stepped out onto the front porch, his eyes blacker than death. At his side stood Camille, her hands limp at her sides, blank eyes staring straight ahead as James held her under his control.

James stopped, his possessed body a stick figure in the blade of light, and looked right at Frank. Tucked in his belt, Camille's Bowie knife glinted in the light. The thin, dark line of a gash ran down his right cheek, dried blood staining his collar.

"Ah, Mr. Butcher!" Frank halted, Spike and Mills spreading out from his sides, weapons ready. "Good to see you, but you're too late. In just a few seconds, my slaves here will light their fuses, and this building will come down on your important gentlemen, and a large number of innocent women.

"I've arranged a special greeting for you, Frank. All the people you see in this yard are under my control, each of them ready to kill you on my command. And since I know how much you like killing women, I made them a mix of my men and students from this college. To get to me, you'll have to kill every one of them, women included. Even your girlfriend, here."

Frank cursed. He could end this with one shot, sending Jesse James back to Hell if he was closer and had the right bullet loaded.

"You think starting the civil war all over again will bring your family's honor back?" Frank shot, hoping to buy time. Spike and Mills continued moving north and south, trying to get in position to stop the dynamite. "It won't bring back your half-brother, won't give Zee back her arm."

James laughed, and lightning struck the dome over his head, thunder shattering the night air.

"You think this is about my family's honor, Butcher? You believe I broke out of Hell for something so petty? You're smarter than that, Frank. This is much bigger, and you know it.

"This is your last chance, Butcher," he bellowed, raising his arms. With a single snap of motion, every person in the yard raised their weapon and took aim at Frank and his friends. "Join me. I could use someone like you. It's that, or die."

Frank's gun-hand twitched, his fingers brushing the ivory handle as he squinted up at the body Jesse James possessed. The boy's body had shrunk in on itself, his arms little more than sticks, his black eyes sunken. His joints had turned knobby and bulbous, while the sinew of his limbs held taught with tension, ready to snap any instant.

Frank studied the distance — still too far.

"I died once," Frank spat at the killer's feet, "and I ain't scared of doing it again."

He drew.

Gunfire erupted like a thousand cracks of thunder as the women opened fire. Frank dove for the ground, gunning down the two nearest enemies with deadly precision. To his right and left, Mills and Spike opened fire too, and more dress-clad figures went down in heaps of cloth and hair, rain and blood. The deep boom of the Sharps even split the night air, as Stan added to the volley of lead.

Bullets tore into Frank, rocking him with their impacts, but he no longer cared. His body was a mere tool, a vessel through which he'd been sent to do a job, to retrieve a prisoner. Once that job was done, his use for the body would end and his own soul would follow his prey back to Hell.

Frank moved forward at a deliberate pace, losing sight of Spike and Mills, edging up the hill toward James on the porch. Shooting and reloading, killing and killing some more. Around him, men and women alike screamed, differentiated only by the pitch of their terrorized cries. Each agonizing wail stabbed at Frank's heart like a knife, piercing his confidence and impaling his very being with cold, dull steel. By the time he reached the foot of the steps, he'd lost count of how many he'd killed, but he knew the rain washed away a good amount of his blood. He ignored the holes in his chest, arms and legs. They hurt, but they would heal, and he wouldn't need his body after this anyway.

He stood at the base of the marble steps, slick with blood and rain, littered with bodies, and glared up at Jesse James.

"Now, you're coming with me."

But James stared off into the darkness to Frank's right, like the gunfighter didn't exist, eyes wide.

That's when Frank heard the growl.

HELL'S MARSHAL

CHAPTER SEVENTEEN

A mass of fur and teeth careened into him before Frank could react, knocking him off his feet and sending his pistol sliding away. He landed with a crunch on the wet, hard ground, his left shoulder separating, firing a burst of pain down his arm and into the fingers.

Yellow eyes glared down at him as the Hellhound landed on top of him, its jaws clamping down with brutal force on his left forearm. The beast shook its head, and Frank cried out as old, long-dead bones snapped, tendons tore, and flesh shredded. The beast picked him up by the arm, shaking him like a piece of meat ripped from a carcass.

An instant later, he flew through the air and landed with a splash on the muddy hillside. Pain roared where his arm had been torn off, leaving a jagged stump of bone below the elbow, blood pulsing from the wound. He waited for his body to fix itself, but nothing happened. Perhaps he'd reached the limits of re-animation, but blood continued to flow, pain burning.

Frank forced himself to his knees. His six-shooter sat a few feet away, so he picked it up with his remaining hand. The Hellhound still shook the chunk of his arm in its jaws, oblivious in its bloodlust to his presence. Frank spun the cylinder open on his pistol and dumped six empty shells onto the ground. His ammo belt held only one more round: his last coated bullet.

He felt eyes on him, and looked up to find the Hellhound stalking closer. It tossed aside the severed stub of his arm, growling and showing bright, dripping, yellow fangs.

Frank held his pistol between his knees and fed the bullet into the cylinder, slapping the gun back into one piece. If he used the bullet on the Hellhound, he'd have nothing but the cuffs with which to handle James, but if he didn't, he'd die before he could take the bandit back to Hell.

He brought the gun up in his right hand, aiming at the hellhound's head. The beast stalked closer, jaws snapping, eyes glowing with yellow malice through the drenching rain. Frank pulled back the hammer, braced himself, and—

A dark shape streaked over Frank's shoulder with a fierce snarl, barreling into the hound and driving it backward. The two tumbled across the ground, splashing through puddles, silhouettes against the flashes of lightning that lit up the night sky.

A second creature growled now, a fierce but earthy sound punctuated with the snapping of teeth. Then came a sickening crunch, a tearing sound, and a long, hissing gurgle. The Hellhound lay still on the grass, fur matted with mud and blood, as a smaller creature stalked toward Frank. Its eyes didn't glow, and when it dropped the Hellhound's ripped-out throat at Frank's feet, he knew it meant him no harm.

Batcho nudged the destroyed chunk of flesh toward Frank, his tongue lolling out to one side as blood dripped from his lips. He yipped.

"I guess you're useful, after all."

Batcho growled again, but this time, his eyes focused up the steps.

"What a pleasant surprise that was," James hissed. "Now, you die together."

Frank turned, pain throbbing up the remains of his arm and into his shoulder, to find James staring down at him from behind Camille. The killer held his pistol to Camille's head, and Frank knew he couldn't shoot the bandit without hitting the hooker.

"See, gunfighter," James mocked, "to kill me, you have to kill two kinds of people you can't stand killing: a woman and a child."

Frank studied the situation, taking in every angle. His consciousness was fading, his vision wavering. Spike lay in a crumpled heap to his right, the extinguished dynamite clutched to his chest. To the left, Mills was nowhere to be seen, and one dress-wearing gang member knelt and lit the dynamite fuse. It sparked and sputtered in the rain.

Camille's eyes remained blank, but her jaw had clenched, as if she were straining against a great force. Yet, she still stood in front of Jesse James.

James was right—Frank would have to kill Camille and Jeb Fisher to do what he'd been sent to do. And even that might not be enough to send the robber back to Hell.

He holstered his gun.

James laughed his serpentine, mocking laugh. "Ha! I knew you couldn't kill a child! You've gone soft, Butcher. You're as worthless a marshal as you were a father."

The words hit like hammers, knocking Frank to his knees while Jesse James tossed his head back and laughed. In that instant, Camille's blank stare changed, as if she'd broken James' control. She blinked hard, looked Frank right in the eye, and nodded.

That gave him hope, and, with hope, came an idea.

A shot rang out to his left. It took him a moment to realize he'd been hit, but when he felt tightness in his chest, he looked down to see blood seeping through a hole in his duster. Pain hit him hard, making him gasp and causing bubbles to sputter in the blood. The shooter fell, a shot from the Sharps reaching Frank a split second later, but Stan was too late.

Frank fell on his face in the dirt. As darkness swirled around him, threatening to drag him into its depths forever, he heard a voice. It sounded distant, across a great sea maybe, but he knew it. It had haunted him for years.

Pa, get up, it pleaded. *You can't give up. They need you.*

"Ron?" Frank whispered, forcing his eyes to remain open.

Kill him, Pa. It's what he needs.

Then the voice was gone, echoing through him, urging him to do what needed done, offering something Frank had never expected: forgiveness.

Gathering the last scraps of his strength, Frank vaulted to his feet and sprinted up the hill, angling left, keeping James in sight. The robber turned, keeping Camille between them. Frank needed to be closer, but the fuse burned short. Time was running out.

Finally, when he couldn't get any closer, Frank threw the cuffs. Camille snatched the steel bracelets out of the air and snapped one on Jeb Fisher's wrist where he held her throat. The boy's black eyes widened, but he didn't loosen his grip, and a moment later, he laughed.

"You still can't kill her."

"She's already dead," Frank growled.

He drew and fired.

James' head snapped back as Camille spun to the right. A trickle of blood rolled down his forehead, dripping from his right eyebrow onto his cheek, and smoke rose from a hole just above his right eye. But he didn't fall.

He wiped the blood on the back of his hand and looked at it. For a heartbeat, Frank thought he'd failed, that the Holy-whiskey hadn't been enough to kill a creature as strong as James and his rampage through the world of the living would continue.

Then Camille jumped forward, snatched the Bowie from James' belt, and buried it to the hilt in his throat.

"Go to hell, you sonofabitch!"

James staggered backward, and for a moment, his black eyes turned blue in the light of the doorway. Frank expected Jeb Fisher to look scared, but instead, his features relaxed and he looked...relieved. Then the obsidian returned to his eyes, and the corners of his mouth angled down.

"This ain't over, Butcher."

With that, he toppled over, a swirling cloud of green light engulfing him, dragging James' soul from Jeb Fisher's body and back to the depths of Hell faster than Frank expected. The body that hit the ground was once again just a boy.

Camille faced Frank and smiled for an instant, but

blood streamed down her neck where Frank's bullet had passed through before hitting James. She gave Frank a helpless look, then collapsed on top of Jeb Fisher.

Frank forced his legs to move toward the dynamite at the north corner of the building, right under the window where Crittenden and Pinkerton met, but he knew he couldn't do it. He wasn't fast enough. He collapsed to his knees beside the crumpled form of a man in a dress, a shotgun by his side.

A figure rose from the hillside, and a flash of lightning showed a bowler on its head. Mills grabbed the dynamite, hugged it to his chest, and dove down the hill just as the explosion shook the earth.

Frank bowed his head. In the distance, Stan's stagecoach barreled toward him, the driver's blue eyes slicing through the night like beacons. Beside him rode Curtis, and for an instant, Ron's voice whispered in his mind again.

He needs a father.

The voice reminded Frank why he'd been in Hell in the first place. Ron had died at his hands, a life cut short by one bent on violence.

Frank looked around at the bodies littering the hillside. How many innocent women had he killed? And he'd killed the boy Jeb Fisher, too. Once a killer, always a killer.

Curtis deserved better. If he grew up with Frank as a father figure, he'd end up just like him — a murderer. And now, more than ever, Frank deserved Hell.

Frank picked up the shotgun and put the barrel under his chin. From the speeding stage, Curtis screamed, and Stan reined in, hugging the boy close, shielding his eyes.

Knowing Curtis was in good hands, Frank pulled the trigger.

EPILOGUE

Frank stood before the judges' long table in Hell again as the three shadowy figures in dusters marched into the dark room, and stood behind the table. Flames shot higher against the back wall as if angered by their presence.

As always, their eyes glowed: blue on the right, green on the left, and a spiteful red of hate in the middle, where Judge John Webber stood, arms crossed over his chest.

"You did what we asked." Webber's voice sounded less than pleased.

"Despite your lies and omissions, yes."

Pain exploded in his temples, driving him to his knees. When it relented, Webber hissed a laugh.

"Learn your place, Marshal."

"You should have told me about the prospector." Frank struggled to his feet. "And that damned Hellhound. How did they know where to find me?"

The judges conferred in their snake-hiss voices.

"We do not know," they said, as one.

"Kinda what I thought," Frank muttered. Webber's eyes narrowed. He was hiding something, Frank knew, not that it mattered now. "I held up my end of the bargain, now — "

The steel-bound double doors behind him boomed open, allowing Camille and Spike to enter. Camille glared at Frank as she passed.

"What's up your petticoats?" Frank snarled at her. "You told me to take the shot."

"I thought you'd shoot around me, not through me!" A bullet hole oozed blood in the nape of her throat, and her voice whistled and gurgled. "Now I'm back here again, you jackass."

"Silence!" Webber bellowed. "Jesse James' soul has been returned to Hell, true, but not without extensive chaos and death in the world of the living. We had to pull the wool over The Boss's eyes, which ain't easy to do. You violated the second part of our agreement.

"However, you did prevent James from advancing his plan, and saved the lives of several innocents, so the court imposes the following sentences. Camille Logan and Stephen "Spike" Miller, your suffering will be reduced by half."

Camille looked visibly relieved, and even Spike relaxed, his shoulders slumping and his fists unclenching.

"What about Mills?" Frank asked. "He died doing good."

The judges conferred a moment before answering.

"Charles Mills faces tests in his own underworld now to determine his eternal fate. Your guide is helping him."

Frank felt a tinge of pity for the detective. Those would be difficult tests. Painful. And Batcho would be little help.

"Now, Frank Butcher, we will reduce your punishment by a quarter, since you did kill an exceedingly large number of innocent people, and were belligerent before this court."

Frank pointed at Webber, taking a half-step forward before remembering the explosion of pain the man could cause.

"Way I see it," he growled, "I killed innocent women

and put a slug between the eyes of a fourteen year old boy. I deserve more pain. That was our deal."

Webber dropped his hands to his side, brushing aside his duster to reveal a six-shooter holstered there, a green glow surrounding it. His threat went unspoken, but Frank heard it clearly, nonetheless.

"Like I said," Webber replied, his voice dropping as his eyes smoldered, "you failed in half of your assigned tasks and needed us to bail you out of trouble, so the deal is void."

Rage coursing through him, Frank fought the urge to rush the figure and wrap his fingers around his throat. The green glow of Webber's gun held his temper in check—if his soul was destroyed, his suffering would end and atonement would halt forever. So he stood, fists clenched, fuming at the judges.

He'd done things just as bad as his original sins, yet somehow, he was destined to suffer less. Fists bunched at his sides, Frank managed to suppress the rage flowing through his body. They'd set him up to fail, manipulated him from the start, and in the end, they still got their way. Frank had inched closer to forgiveness he didn't deserve.

The judges filed out of the room, but just before he left, Webber stopped and looked Frank in the eye.

"Don't worry too much, Marshal. You'll have other chances. The position of Hell's Marshal is appointed for eternity."

Webber started to go, but Frank wasn't done.

"James didn't know about the Hellhound."

Webber stopped, his back to Frank. "He must have."

"He didn't. What do you suppose that means, Judge?"

Webber shot a baleful red glare over his shoulder. "Means you're very lucky."

As the oily judge disappeared, Frank remembered

the final words of Jesse James' spirit as it was sucked back to the depths of Hell.

This ain't over, Butcher.

Somehow, Frank knew he was right.